RW

9

**Norman
Baxter**

TYE TWOLFBAY

Know the game?

Prince digs a rebound out of a crowd in front of the Annapolis goalie and fires the puck back to Dooby at the point. Dooby winds up and one-times a slapper six inches off the ice. Somehow it eludes the tangle of legs and ankles and comes in on goal. The goalie sees it and moves his stick to block, but Cody, who would be skating through the crease, lifts his skates and while in the air tips the puck, redirecting it above the stick and into the net. Then he lands, with one skate in the crease. Goal?

Woodsie
Zip
Cody
Boot
Prince
Shark
Billy
Dooby...

(and more next season . . .)

THE WOLFBAY Wings

by **BRUCE BROOKS**
available in paperback

📚 **HarperTrophy**

Boot

Boot knows his own game: He scores from in close, and his swings at the puck are usually quick, choppy, and opportunistic. So the Boot very carefully uses only a stick with an absolutely straight blade: Thus his forehand and backhand have equal sweet spots, though his forehand wristers lack that snap a curved stick gives.

Art © 1998 by Erik Butler

Goal. Unless his skate is *on* the ice in the crease, and as long as he was not pushed there by a defensive player, and the puck did not precede him into the crease, then he may touch it and score. Jumping off the ice counts.

Shafted

The Montrose center is a kid who *used* to be my friend. We set for the face-off. I ignore the puck as it drops and snap my stick's heel down hard on the spot where the aluminum shaft of his glitzy model attaches to the wooden blade. The joint pops. They always pop if you hit them right. The guy is left staring at his nice sixty-dollar metal shaft as I kick the puck wide to Barry out on the left wing.

We kill the clock without letting Moseby touch the puck. The buzzer ends it. As the rest of the guys whoop it up, I skate by the kid holding his shaft.

"I been brought up to expect colored people to use cheap tricks," he says. "I should have known."

"If you want to talk about something you should have known, then maybe you should have known your own equipment, Caucasian. Never take a big face-off with one of those tin sticks."

"This used to be *our* sport," he says as I skate off. I laugh.

PRINCE

PRINCE

BRUCE BROOKS

A LAURA GERINGER BOOK

HarperTrophy®
A Division of HarperCollinsPublishers

Prince
Copyright © 1998 by Bruce Brooks

Library of Congress Cataloging-in-Publication Data
Brooks, Bruce.
    Prince / Bruce Brooks.
        p.   cm. — (Wolfbay Wings ; #5)
    "A Laura Geringer book."
    Summary: When Prince, the Wolfbay Wings' only black
hockey player, is aggressively recruited to play for the basket-
ball team, he is torn between the sport he and his grandfather
know and love and the sport that everyone else thinks he
ought to play.
    ISBN 0-06-440600-8 (pbk.) — ISBN 0-06-027542-1 (lib. bdg.)
    [1. Hockey—Fiction.   2. Basketball—Fiction.   3. Afro-
Americans—Fiction.   Grandfathers—Fiction.]   I. Title.
II. Series: Brooks, Bruce.   Wolfbay Wings ; #5.
PZ7.B7913Pr 1998   97-40265
[Fic]—dc21   CIP
                                                          AC

Typography by Steve Scott
1   2   3   4   5   6   7   8   9   10
❖
First Edition
Visit us on the World Wide Web!
http://www.harperchildrens.com

PRINCE

am panting like a dog running from a rainstorm as I barely make it to the bench and bang through the next line of players going out, and *they* make it all the more bangy because they have to try to clang us on the shoulders and helmets and say nice things and stuff. I finally reach my spot and flop down on my pants and hang my head, sucking at the air. It was a long shift. Best shift I ever had, but *long*.

Dooby, however, seems fresh as a new puddle. He drops down next to me and shoves the butt end of his stick, all nasty with black-edged adhesive tape he hasn't changed since our first tie-up, against my face mask.

"And—yes, Phil, am I—?" I sneak a look up and see he's holding his other hand to his off-ear the way those color-guys on the Deuce do, "—yes, okay—" He puts on a big fake grin and turns to me. "We're here with the man they call Prince," he says, "and, heh heh, I don't think I'd be stretching it to say he just had himself a *king*-sized shift out there against this highly favored Squirt-A team from Montrose. Now, just for the record, Your Highness—I *may* call you Your Highness, may I not?"

"You better," I pant.

"Right!" He fake-smiles. "Now, as I say, just for the record—*how* many assists *did* you amass during that single shift? The princely number of two, was it not?"

It was three. "Four," I say.

His eyebrows shoot up and he makes as if he's hearing something over his earphone. "My statisticians must have missed one, heh heh. They have you down for three and since that's the number of goals your team actually scored—"

"But I got two on Cody's second, see. Two assists on one goal." You can't get two on one, of course.

"Two on a single goal?" He frowns.

I nod. Before I can start to speak, Woodsie hipchecks Montrose's star center Kenny Moseby and jacks him a foot off the ice, pins him up there long enough for the puck to skitter back to our winger backchecking, then pulls away to let

Moseby fall in a heap. Dooby and I both holler at Woodsie. Moseby doesn't fall in a heap very often.

"Where were we?" Dooby says, shoving his stick back at me.

"I passed it to Cody. He passed it back to me and I shot, but Cheerios got it with a pad and Cody snapped in the 'bound. Now, the rules say the last two men on the scoring team to *pass* the puck—"

"Is it your Canadian heritage that allows you to collect such a gaudy statistic as three assists on one shift, Mr. Prince, sir? You *are* Canadian, yes? Even French-Canadian, if I am not mistaken?

"Mais oui."

"Does this give you that little extra edge—ha ha, skates have an edge, see, ha ha—over your relatively latecoming American counterparts *watch the cherry picker!"*

Moseby was hanging out at the red line and his defenseman knew it and flung the puck up the boards behind our D and it should be a breakaway, except Woodsie was playing pretty far back and gets enough of an angle on Moseby that he can mess with Kenny's stick from behind, and Moseby only gets off what is for *him* a half-decent shot. That is to say, a ripping high one, looks like a speeding dime, headed for the very edge inside the far corner but Zip throws up his blocker and Woodsie beats Moseby to his own rebound.

"Not *that* particular American," I say, pointing to Kenny.

"Yes, well, Kenny is what *we* down here call 'special,'" says Dooby. "Speaking of which—how can you read defensemen so well, Mr. Prince? You seem to know how they are going to move, what passing lanes they are going to open up for you, before—ha ha!—they themselves do! Now is *that* perhaps where your hypersensitive rhythmic African-American naturally-improvisatory instincto-athletic voodoo jazz-from-New-Orleans gift comes into play?"

"Yassuh," I say. "It sho' be."

"Thank you." He pulls the stick-end back. On the ice, Moseby almost picks off a sloppy pass to break in alone on Zip, whom he usually eats alive. If K weren't being double-shifted he would have had the legs. But if he weren't being double-shifted, he might not have been out there to try.

"This politically sensitive interview with our international . . ."

I let Dooby fade out. I am in fact tired. It is the third period of an away game against our most hated rivals and we *did* just get three goals on one shift, two by Cody and one by Dooby himself, to stun everybody and take a three-goal lead. The fact that we had been tied, with only four minutes left in the game, was shocking enough. Montrose is an awesome hockey machine, put together player by player with keen loving care by their coach, Marco, who stole our best four or five players from last year—including Kenny—as part of his scheme. They have lost only one game, to a team from Philadelphia, in OT. They beat us by one goal the first time we played them, a great showing for us that was the turnaround in our season. Frankly, even though we've only won a handful since then, we knew we'd kick their tails today.

It's my line's turn, out for the last shift of the game. Marco has rested Kenny for a shift but now has him at left wing, where he is playing opposite Boot, our slowest player, but one of our smartest. But even with double the smarts, Boot won't even know where Kenny went to in three seconds.

"Think you'll get three *this* time?" sneers the Montrose center, a kid named Jon who *used* to be a friend of mine until he jumped ship.

"Probably not," I say. I look up at the scoreboard, where it says 6–3, us. "Think *you* will?"

"No prob," he says, and promptly wins the face-off from me. The defenseman dumps, Moseby beats Dooby to the puck between the corner and the cage and—I swear it's intentional, believe me, he's that kind of kid—snaps a blind backhander high off the middle of Zip's back while Zip, facing forward, watches helplessly over his shoulder. Of course the puck topples into the net. 6–4.

"That's one," says the center, as we set again for the face-off. He checks the clock. "Took eight seconds."

"Yeah, but you cheated," I say, as the ref shows the puck.

"How so?"

"You held on to your stick," I say, ignoring the puck as it drops and snapping my stick's heel down hard on the spot where the aluminum shaft of his glitzy model attaches to the wooden blade. The joint pops. They always pop if you hit them right. The guy is left staring at his nice sixty-dollar metal shaft as I kick the puck wide, away from Moseby's side, to Barry out on the left wing. He works it to Cody and I leave the other center deciding whether to get another stick from the bench or haul me down. He grabs my sleeve, but he waited too long. I'm gone. Cody works it in three-on-two perfect until Moseby hustles back to even it out as Codes whips it to was-open-just-a-*second*-ago me, but I drop it between my legs hoping Dooby is trailing. He is. He winds up, fakes a huge slapshot, two defensemen drop to the ice, but Doobs just skates with the puck behind the net and all the way down the boards to the other end, where he stops dead with it behind Zip. Nobody but Marco has figured out yet that Dooby's more interested in killing time than scoring, so it takes them a while to get in and forecheck and by then he has plenty of us to play catch with, and we kill out the clock without letting Moseby touch the puck. At least three times we pass it right by the bladeless center, who can't stop it with his bladeless shaft.

The buzzer ends it. As the rest of the guys

whoop it up—hey, we *hate* these jerks, and it's only their *second* loss—I skate by the kid holding his shaft. It's kind of a light purple, and it has a famous center's signature painted on it.

"You can have a new blade installed on that baby in fifteen minutes," I say. "Good as new. Be calling you 'Mess' next game for sure."

"I been brought up to expect colored people to use cheap tricks," he says. "I should have known."

"I been brought up to expect colored people to use *smart* tricks," I say. "And if you want to talk about something you should have known, then maybe you should have known your own equipment, Caucasian. Never take a big face-off with one of those tin sticks."

"This used to be *our* sport," he says, as I skate off.

I laugh. He doesn't know what he's talking about too many ways to mess with—I wish he could hear Dooby's interview. I want to go rub Zip's facemask and sing a couple of cool songs in the locker room and throw a little balled-up tape at Dooby's big head. And I want to review those three assists—two of them backhand, just past defenders

I held eye-contact with, one of the passes threaded through *two* sets of Montrose legs to Cody at the corner of the net. I needn't worry about that part, though. My French Canadian grandfather, who has never missed even one of my *practices*, will tell me all about them in the car home. In detail. In French. Hey, I love America, I talk the talk here, but I have to tell you—hockey rules, and not only that, it just sounds better in French, *tu sais?*

was born in Montreal, spoke nothing but French until I was four, when my parents died in a ferry fire. I moved to Baltimore to live with my grandfather. He was from Montreal too and we still never spoke anything but French in the house, but I went to school in Baltimore and learned all kinds of English.

By "all kinds" I mean it. I am black, and in Baltimore every black kid speaks at least three kinds of English: school English, badass-English meant to be overheard, and kick-back-rebel English that can be more private. I am very weak on the latter two, because first of all I don't get the badass thing too well, and second, because switching back and forth from French to English keeps me so serious about words that I don't really find it easy to cut loose and get sloppy.

I am maybe a little stiff for an American city kid. I'm one of those guys people are always calling "such a little man!," embarrassing things like that. If they say it in front of my friends, or even worse my enemies, it's pretty nasty.

It's a little different when people say I remind them of my grandfather, this is meant as a compliment and that's how I take it, even though my grandfather is very old and has a first name no one in town can pronounce (Jean-Lucien) and is known frequently to burst into song, full-throated and with rigid vibrato, the song always a standard ballad or a dance tune from bygone days of big band swing, right in the middle of the sidewalk or store for no apparent reason whatever. It so happens that I sing too—it so happens that I even sing standard ballads and dance tunes from the swing era as taught to me by my grandfather. But it *never* happens that I do so out of the blue, in public.

Even though he has been known to startle a shoe salesman or a news vendor with a quick verse of "How High the Moon?," my grandfather is much appreciated in our town of Severna Park as a perfect gentleman. He is a very dignified figure, thin and sharp and stylish. He is very handsome, with features, such as a blade nose and high cheekbones, that I believe are often called "European" (which means "He doesn't look especially African!"); his posture stands him upright and proud. Always there is an air about him of being in some way on display—not at all like he is showing off, nothing so vulgar, just a presence that realizes it will draw attention.

He comes by this well. For most of his life his job was largely to draw attention. In the 1930s and 40s he was in fact a jazz singer (and dancer: He was the first swing singer to take the microphone off its stand and choreograph his movements to a song), spending seven years with the Duke Ellington Orchestra at one time, the top of the top. All of the songs were in English, and for a long time he didn't know any more of the language than the rhyming lyrics of romance. He met my grandmother in a ballroom during a break from an Ellington concert, and to talk to her he used the only language he knew. She thought he was incredibly cool and married him the next day. Later, after he came back and settled in Baltimore, she found out the truth. She taught him the rest of English pretty fast. But they raised my father in both languages, and sent him to prep school and college in Montreal, where he remained and got married to my mom, and they lucked out and had me.

He'd been lonely after my grandmother died, and so when I lost my parents, he was anxious to bring me to The States. He wanted me to become almost entirely an American. However, he wanted me to remain partly Canadian— French Canadian, Montreal-born—in some way that I could be *proud* of, forever. There had to be something of Canada that I could keep alive. My grandfather always said he made three big sacrifices in coming to this country: They made terrible *bread* here, they made terrible *coffee*, and they made terrible conversation about *sport*, because they had nothing but terrible sports to talk about. He knew he wouldn't teach me to spend my time baking, he knew I was too young to worry much about coffee. But he decided I was just the right age to fix the sport problem. So, instead of letting me out into the streets and playgrounds to play basketball and football and baseball with my buddies, he bought me a pair of ice skates and located all of the city's ancient dingy ice rinks down secret alleys and out near dark wharves, and he got me skating and set about teaching me what he, like any Canadian, thought was the only worthy sport in the world: Hockey.

I love to play ice hockey. There are many ways in which no other game compares to it, for speed, creativity, roughness, and pure absolute cool. When I was five I was already good, and my grandfather tried to start a club in some of those Baltimore rinks so I could get some competition, but all he found were basketball leagues in the gymnasiums everywhere. Later that year we moved to a town near Annapolis, and here he found five different ice hockey clubs, one of which I joined. I have played travel hockey here for years now. I'm fairly excellent at passing the puck. (You are allowed to brag a little if you are a passer. A goal scorer who brags is kind of a jerk.)

Do I sound like a person who has too much pride? Perhaps I do. But you can see from what I have mentioned that I have a lot to be proud of. The trouble is, I have even *more* to be proud of, stuff I haven't mentioned yet, and another, different kind of pride. And that's the part I don't really know what to do with.

three

"**P**rince! Circle!"

I am being pushed hard into the boards from behind by a grunting Rockville defenseman who weighs fifty pounds more than me but has fifty points less on his IQ, because instead of getting his stick down on the ice where he might be able to dig the puck out of the corner and away, he continues to hold it up high in both hands so he can cross-check me again and again in the shoulder blades, like a rough guy. I hear Cody's holler, so the next time Rocky draws his stick back to wind up for the cross-check, I splay my skates out backwards and to the sides. Each of my skates catches the inside of each of Rocky's, and suddenly without meaning to, he opens up his five-hole nice and wide, losing his balance too. While he waves his arms to stay up, I shorten my hands on my stick, turn the blade between the puck and the dasher, and snap a real beauty of a blind backhand back between all four legs, just to where Cody must be as he follows the arc of the face-off circle. Rocky falls just then, and grabs my neck to take me with him. He makes sure he lands on me and shoves my head into the ice, but I hear the roar. Cody must have scored.

"It's all in the brains," I tell Rocky, tapping his helmet with my glove as we lie, face mask to face mask.

"You lucky fudgesicle," he says. "Why aren't you out playing basketball with your pants around your knees like the rest of your soul brothers?"

"Because I'd rather be in here humiliating you." The linesman arrives and separates us, and as soon as he's certain he's restrained, the Rockville moron pretends to struggle and jab at me.

I sigh. "But maybe you're right," I say. "Humiliating the likes of you is getting to be all too easy."

At that moment Cody skates by, hooks my left skate out from under me, and hollers, "Great look, Princer!" as I hit the ice.

"I wasn't *looking!* That's the *genius* of it!" I yell back, climbing to my skates and heading to the bench. I check the scoreboard. Cody's goal put us up 5–2, with four minutes to go. If we hold on, this will be our third win in a row, the best streak of this season.

My teammates smack my helmet as I skate by to the bench gate, muttering my name, complimenting my pass. Hockey players, more than any athletes I have ever run across, are hip to the good pass. No sport honors passes the way hockey does in terms of individual glory statistics. When a goal is scored, the last two offensive players to touch the puck before the goal scorer receive "assists," which count exactly the same as goals in the overall total of a player's scoring.

Mostly, though, hockey players just get the *idea* of passing. For one thing it's what makes this game so incredibly fast. For another, you can make your passes a lot flashier than your shots. Nobody would ever *shoot* the puck from the boards backwards between the legs blind, the way I just did, for example. Also, as it has always occurred to me, a guy carrying the puck has five options if he wants to pass, but only one if he wants to shoot. And hockey players love to be unpredictable.

As I turn in the gate Coach Cooper pats my shoulder and says, "Good skatework, Frenchy." Coach Cooper sometimes refuses to call me by my team nickname, which is Prince. Nicknames on a hockey team are pretty simple things. If, for example, you have a large nose, your nickname is going to be Nose. If your skating pace is the slowest on the team, almost certainly you will be called Speedy. I am a short black person who sings all the time, so, of course, to these MTV-watching white kids I am Prince. My grandfather thinks Prince refers to a royalty status, not to a weird guy from Minneapolis with a nasty falsetto. Nobody has told him. The guys on the team are really nice to my grandfather, though all he ever says to them is that they should skate harder and pass more quickly. But he says it in French, so they don't care.

I have noticed that Coach Cooper carefully avoids rubbing my helmet, which is the most natural move in the hockey world to congratulate someone. It took me a long time before I found out from a radical dude at school that black people were supposed to consider it an outrage when white people rubbed them on the head, because back in the days of slavery or perhaps more recently, fat white racist pigs with diamond pinky rings would call the broken-spirited people of color who worked for them into the room and rub their woolly heads "for luck." I wouldn't have minded if Coach rubbed mine—everyone else did—but my grandfather noticed that Coach did *not*, and it meant something to the old man: He always called Coach Cooper (in French) "that very sensitive gentleman."

Dooby, a defenseman, skates up hard behind me and stops, bumping me through the gate. "What's it gonna be?" he says, cocking a head at the scoreboard. As we sit, I pretend to study it with a frowning, thoughtful air. By now Dooby isn't the only one waiting; several other players are watching me. "We'll get eight," I finally say. "And they're stuck where they are." Dooby whoops and says "It's all over now," others nod, we all turn our attention back to the ice. As we watch, Zip blocks a nice rising wrist shot from the right circle, juggles the rebound, catches it in his mitt, tosses it in the air in front of him, and, with both hands on his stick, swats it as if he were Ken Griffey, Jr. Off the fly it lands just inside the far blue line, and actually trickles in on goal. We can all hear the referee holler at Zip to stop hot-dogging.

"Why?" Zip asks.

The ref cannot think of an answer.

Almost every ref in the league would probably pick Zip as the goaltender he is least fond of. I can think of only one ref who thinks otherwise—a man named Sparky who shows up for most games not quite drunk enough to be turned away: He is easily the best skater in the whole area, and no one can help liking him as he speeds around the rink, cheeks flushed, longish gray hair flying behind him, body twisting and turning as he slips through impossibly small spaces that close a second later, all to get a better view of the play. The players love Sparky for three reasons: First, he warns you before he whistles you ("If you keep getting that stick of yours up on his hands I'm gonna have to nail you!"); second, after a game he often seeks out kids he has called penalties on, to shake hands and teach them the legal way to do what they were trying to accomplish illegally; third, and most important, he gets closer to the nitty-gritty action of the game *without* interfering. Great passes are never spoiled by hitting

Sparky's skates, clear shots up the boards are never bounced back into the zone off Sparky's legs.

And he *loves* Zip. He calls him "Spunk." Zip, true to character, calls Sparky "Johnnie Walker Red."

Two goals to go to make my prediction. On the ice, with his back to the goal, Ernie feels a clearing pass hit him on the rear. Without pausing he spins neatly on his skates and swings his stick where the dropping puck probably *ought* to be. It is, and he connects, and the flat shot knuckleballs its way through the Rockies and the goalie's pads. Ernie, howling, tries to run on his skate tips with his hands in the air, but falls to his knees. Coach calls for a fresh shift; the Rockville guys are hanging their heads.

Our team this year has developed a peculiar kind of advantage. We started the season being so unbelievably bad that some teams were practically ashamed to play us (I said "practically"—they all found it in their hearts to go ahead and pulverize us anyway). Then we kind of pulled things together, a couple of iffy guys became solid players, freeing the best skaters to play without the pressure of carrying the whole team every shift, and Zip turned into the hottest goalie in the league, and the most vilely hated. Zip seems to invent the *idea* of stopping pucks from going in the cage, *every shot*, every night. A shooter bearing in on Zip can never know what he will see—a goalie on his knees in the slot, a goalie skating hard right at him with his stick in the air, a goalie spinning on his skates in the crease.

Even if the other team gets him way out of position with some pretty fake, then, as their shot is buzzing in on the empty net, some part of Zip's body appears out of nowhere and knocks the puck away.

But even though we have Zip, most teams feel they should beat us. Generally, they have good reason to feel this way, and, generally, they *do* beat us. Hockey is a low scoring game, so most intense action—and every second of a hockey game is a moment of intense action—does not lead to scoring, unlike the way a steal leads to a bucket in basketball or a dropped fly leads to a run in baseball. Still, players can tell from each small challenge, each nearly meaningless confrontation or scramble, that one team is superior to the other— sometimes *way* superior. Some of our players are comically naive about the little tricks of hockey—they stink, in other words—and others can barely skate in their positions. I would be surprised if there has ever been a team that inspires smugness in its opponents as quickly as we do each game.

Ah—but then, what happens when the results don't quite support the smugness? When a team finds it can't quite shake us off? *Then* it's self-doubt time for the other guys.

My shift is the second one in the third period. Their goalie whaps a weak shot from Boot (who was hooked pretty badly) into the corner, and I go after it with the same Rockie who beat on me before. This time he holds up for a second, deciding how to play it, and gives me just enough room to get the puck in my skates. I spin to face him, and, looking him in the eye, kick the puck between his skates. Now he looks down for the puck in the corner and leans forward on his stick, but I jump over the shaft and collect the puck behind him. I cruise in on the net and when the defenseman in the slot refuses to leave Boot and cover me, I take a long look at him, and flip the puck high and shortside, over the goalie's glove-hand shoulder.

I love to make pretty passes. But it feels great to score a goal now and then too.

Woodsie, a defenseman who never played hockey before this season and has developed into one of the smartest players I know, punches my face mask. '"Hey—if the goalie hadn't touched that one to wipe out my pass to Boot, do you know I would tie you for the team lead, Mr. Telepathic Passing Genius?"

I shake my head. "Guess I'll have to pick it up a little, start playing at more than sixty per cent of my capacity the rest of the way." Cody, my left winger, tells me the rotation on my shot was "hideous" to the point that he refuses to count it as a respectable goal, and Coach Cooper sighs when I pass through the gate and says, "It happens to 'em all. One day they like to pass, but the next all they want is to shoot, shoot, shoot."

"That's Boot you're talking about," I say, referring to my right winger, an almost magically gifted goal scorer.

"The Boot has *never* passed," says the Boot. "The Boot *will* never pass." He sits, and I hear him mutter, in a huff, "When the Boot was *born*, he had outgrown the passing stage."

four

ate one afternoon, I go through the swinging double doors to the gym and then turn the knob on the single unmarked door that leads to the locker room of the Severna Middle School Shadows basketball team. The football team is called the Steamrollers, but the hoopsters decided *that* name was far too crude, too thick, too white construction-worker-with-a-hardhat for their sleek, sneaky selves. Several Shadows are stuffing the last items in their gym bags and getting ready to leave when I stick my head in. Three or four look up at me and freeze a dead look on their faces. I pick one kid, a forward named Nicky, and jerk my chin at him in greeting.

"Nick."

" 'S goin', Hoke."

I motion with my head toward the door that leads directly to the court. "Marshall still out?"

"Long as there's a hoop," says Nicky, smiling slightly.

"And a certain coach," I add, with a tense smile of my own. Nicky's smile freezes, the stares of the others get more intense, and for a second there is a serious bit of suspense. Here is why. I am well-known to be the best and in fact the only friend of the very tall, very smart, and very eccentric star center of the Shadows, Marshall Poteet, and I am well-known to come by here every school day to drag him away from basketball practice. The coach is apparently not satisfied, any more than Marshall is, with a scoring average of almost forty points a game and a field-goal percentage of seventy per cent. I am generally regarded as the person who keeps Marshall on the right side of the moon, and, as such, I am tolerated by the coach and by his players.

In addition, I am regularly recruited by the coach to try out for the fearsome Shadows, invited—perhaps "cajoled" says it better—in such a way that when I decline the honor and remind him that my winter sports schedule is taken up with a fifty-five-game ice hockey season, he makes it clear that a black kid who chooses to mess around on ice skates with a bunch of white kids with crew cuts must be either a traitor to his race or a fool. Still, at times the coach does his charming best to make me feel that I could be practically a part of the team. And I know the charm will be on full wattage today—tryouts are tomorrow. But I know that the real team members, with the exception of Marshall, see me more as a kind of spying cockroach.

Now, as sometimes happens with little symbolic things, the privilege of walking through the locker room and out that far door onto the court has become an intimate honor reserved only for Shadows. And every few days, when I stop by, some of them watch me warily lest I make a dash for it and steal a status I have not earned. Weird, but athletes come up with a lot of strange stuff.

I have better sense than to bolt for the precious door. Instead, I wave at the room in general and thank Nicky, then walk up a staircase and out along the top of bleachers that are folded out every day for the spectators who want to watch basketball practice. There are only about twenty-five kids left today, and none of them are paying much attention to the only hoops still going down in the building.

Out on the floor, in the paint beneath one basket, a well-muscled man just over six feet tall, wearing baggy gray shorts and a sleeveless University of Maryland T-shirt so faded that its red has become a pleasant fuzzy pink, is dribbling a ball and talking back over his shoulder to a taller but utterly unmuscled kid wearing green shorts that are pulled up too high, with a plain white undershirt tucked into the waistband, and very large black-framed glasses. This kid is standing straight up, arms at his sides, despite the fact that the other man keeps bumping backwards into his legs while dribbling and talking. This goes on for a while, long enough that it is plain to see that the tall boy is getting so bored he may fall asleep standing up.

Then all of a sudden and with great quickness the man leaps surprisingly high, and spins, and leans far back away from the boy, and launches a high lofting shot at the basket ten feet away.

He never stopped talking, never gave a sign that he was about to do this. Nevertheless, without looking as if he has waked up, the tall boy seems to levitate straight upwards without crouching an inch to collect his muscles for a leap, and slowly one of those previously limp arms unfurls upwards like a black telescope, and on its end a long, delicate hand appears, and this hand gently, almost apologetically stops the ball's arc toward the basket, then catches the ball on the way down.

For a split second, so fast it might almost be imagined, the man's face flashes a look of resentment, but then he grins, and nods, and says, "Okay, good, that's enough for now." He makes for the door to the locker room. The boy, still holding the ball in one hand at chest level, pivots to watch him go to the door. Then the glasses turn toward the bleachers, scan them, and finally stop when they find me. I wave. The boy smiles.

"Marshall!" The coach is holding the door. He flicks a glance my way but continues to stare at the boy. You can see now that the man is pretty tired. The fuzzy pink shirt is colored a wet steak color by sweat all across his chest.

Marshall waves at me with the hand not holding the ball, and motions toward the locker room. I nod. He nods, and smiles again. Then he looks over at the tired coach, and with a sudden jerk half-runs for the door, which he reaches in two strides.

I decide to wait for Marshall outside the locker room. Sometimes his coach—whose name is Clark Weatherspoon, or so it was when he was a second-team All-American guard at the University of Maryland years ago, but who claims to have changed it to something African and insists that selected students call him Kantuu—wants to use up every minute of Marshall's attention, and talks hoops to him until the final shoelace in Marshall's incredibly unstylish brogans is knotted. Coach Kantuu believes that to be a genius, the best player ever to come from the state of Maryland, Marshall needs knowledge, knowledge, knowledge, bestowed in the form of words, words, words. I believe that to be a genius Marshall needs only a basketball in his hands and a hoop. He is already smarter than Coach Kantuu and any other five students in the school put together. It's just that nobody knows it because he doesn't especially like to speak.

To my surprise, the door to the locker room opens and the coach's head sticks out. He sees me and says, "Get in here, okay?"

I walk in, hands in my pockets. "Hey, Marshall," I say.

"Hey, Prince." Marshall is the only school kid who calls me by my hockey-team nickname. I have another nickname at school, given to me by my African-American brother and sisters, and it is not nearly as friendly as Prince. It is "Hokey," a combination of Hoagy (Carmichael, because he sang those old-timey songs), "hockey" (because, incomprehensible though it is, I choose to play this game), and "honky" (because that is who one plays hockey *with*).

"I was telling Marsh here that he has developed the best low-post game in the state at the AAA level, middle *or* high school," the coach says, toweling off and watching Marshall. Marshall says nothing. The coach nods. "I was telling him that with a great low-post game he could make the move back and forth from center to power forward. Much more versatile. Much harder to guard. Much more appealing to those college scouts."

"I'm not going to play basketball in college," says Marshall. I have heard him say it, to Coach Kantuu, at least a hundred times. I have yet to hear Coach Kantuu acknowledge it. "I am going to college to study biochemistry, a curriculum the difficulty of which will not be compatible with the consuming vigors of bigtime sports hoopla."

Towelling his longish, looseish hair, Coach Kantuu shoots me a look. "Only trouble is, Marshall needs someone he can count on to get him the ball down there." I groan. He is playing it casual this time—at others, it ranges from personal-intense (*"You* got what I had, kid—can you imagine what that does for me?") to cultural-shame-redemption ("Lots of The People see you thinking you too *good* to be playing The People's Game . . ."). I am surprised at the light touch today of all days, what with the moment of truth (will he? won't he) coming tomorrow afternoon.

"Now, Coach—"

"And it can't be just any old point guard of course," he talks on. "To get that pass kicked in there deep and proper, you got to have a guard that has penetrated the perimeter of the D, maybe even drawn the forward out a couple of steps so he won't be able to double-team as easy. Not every guard has that kind of instinct, that kind of footwork, that kind of eye—"

Marshall looks at me and raises his shoulders. "Sorry."

"It's okay," I say.

"Tryouts and all."

"Got it." I spent two weeks at a basketball camp about a million years ago and Kantuu won't let me forget it. "My fault, as always, for showing off. Shouldn't pretend to dance if you don't like the music."

Coach Kantuu—unusually, for him—has stopped his speech and is listening as he finishes towelling. "No," he says, "what you *shouldn't* have done is listen to that old Canadian man you got instead of an American daddy who would bring you up right. Him telling you Lord knows *what* about being true to your culture." He chucks the towel onto the floor and fixes me with a Kantuu the Warrior stare. "You gonna wake up one day and see your culture's right *here*." He points to the door to the gym. "Right *there*."

I look at him coldly. "Take it back."

He stares. My fists are curled, loose. I am

crouched perhaps two inches. He knows he would slaughter me but it may not be worth the lawsuit. "Okay, sorry, no disrespect meant, he's a fine old gent, did the best he could, all that. He doesn't know any better."

"And he's not the only Canadian," I say.

"I know, I know"—he sighs wearily and rolls his eyes—"you are a natural-born Quebecois, *oui oui*. Okay. But this is the U.S., my man, and, as you just pointed out, you *did* attend that high rollin' camp that summer at Georgetown and you did play the eyes out of everyone there and so it is nothing but for your *benefit* that I am trying to get you to *fulfill* your awesome potential as a basketball player instead of wasting your life getting into fistfights with canteloupe farmers who drive tractors and wear ice skates."

"Their *parents* are the canteloupe farmers," I say patiently. "The boys themselves are all going for PhD's in biochemistry." I look at Marshall. "You ready?"

"Um . . ." Standing, he looks around for his books. They are under his right arm. Eventually he finds them. "Yeah," he says.

"'Bye, Coach Weatherspoon."

"Good night, Coach."

The coach is standing before a mirror, loosely knotting a necktie made of a thin velour the same shade of deep green as his polished cotton shirt. His eyes in the mirror find mine. "Think about it," he says. "I've been patient with you. Come out tomorrow night, or be lost forever. And don't expect me to keep keeping the Yo kids off your cafe-au-lait back. You have no idea what kind of trouble I've saved you, Skates."

"I can imagine. Ritual circumcision, facial scars, forswearing of auxiliary verbs, feet forced every morning into Reeboks—"

He shakes his head angrily. "If you can joke, you haven't thought about it enough." He finishes the knot, such as it is. Looking around the floor near him, he says, "Marshall. You work your tail off. But you *need* him, Marshall. *Him*. He got any reason to let *you* hang out to dry?" He bends down to shoehorn his bare feet into some loafers made of very thin navy leather.

o Marshall and I are walking home in silence, as we usually do. The wind is picking up, slapping leaves and candy wrappers against our legs.

"You're still mad about what he said," Marshall says softly. "About your grandfather."

I nod.

"Really mad, right?"

I nod again. A Milky Way wrapper sticks to the shin of my jeans and I hop on one foot and tear it away with the other. Hockey player's move.

"He was pretty crude, I have to admit," Marshall says "He's actually a pretty crude man in general, and not all that intelligent. He's a terrible math teacher. But he *is* loyal."

"Look, Marshall—"

"The thing is," Marshall continues, "the funny thing is, you aren't really so mad at *him*, at Coach Weatherspoon. You're mad, you're *really* mad, at yourself. Because you *did* go that camp to spite your grandfather, because for a few days or weeks there, you were thinking almost what the coach just finished saying."

I look up at Marshall. For someone who can't say "hi" to a fourth grader without terror, this was quite a proclamation. With a slight frown he studies the ground directly in front of his size 11 feet, as if he might take a step that would drop him into a social tea or a piano recital or some other milieu that is his personal definition of hell.

"Don't bother to tell me I'm wrong," he says, still softly. He pushes his glasses up his nose. "You know I wouldn't bother to talk unless I was right."

I laugh. "You sure do leave me a lot of options."

"But I'm right?" He looks over at me.

I sigh. "You're right."

It's true. Two summers ago, I suddenly found myself *tired* of being so completely different from all of my friends—tired of being the only one who played hockey instead of hoops, tired of using my perfect pitch and exquisite falsetto to croon "The Impossible Dream" or a drippy Sondheim medley with out-of-tune student orchestras at school assemblies, while my buddies were chillin' in their basements with busted turntables and scratchy records, talking *trash* and making *noise*. Tired of being called "Oreo" and "Hokey" and as one too-downtown girl put it and made it stick for a few months, "Gretzky Noir." So I came home one day in the spring, after the endless travel hockey season had finally ended while everyone else had been out running around in the sunshine, and I walked into his music room, where my grandfather, dressed as always in a sports coat and tie, was sitting at his piano. Sounding as bold as I could I told him that instead of going to ice hockey camp in Toronto that summer I wanted to go to two weeks of basketball camp at George-town University. (It was *the* hoops camp for black kids.)

Of course, his first instinct was to say no, and he nearly did. I was ready for him. But he just managed to hold back, and to sit there with his thin fingers held in the shape of a chord that would never come, and to look me over very carefully, from the black 'X' cap I wore backwards on my shaved head to the ludicrously oversized Raiders jacket hanging open over my ICE-T T-shirt and my butt-draggin' jeans, all the way down to my $150 sneakers (Shawn Kemps? Jason Kidds? Pennys?) with the laces wildly undone. He looked me up and down, and nodded, as if to himself, and he said, "So, where do children stay at this university?"

So I went. And once there, with the Yo kids, I talked it and walked it, spending every hour off the court pretending to like Snoop Dogg and Dr. Dre (instead of say, George Clinton, whom I love), slinking up Wisconsin Avenue after curfew to scare the yuppies out drinking champagne, learning dozens of arcane handshakes and mumbled greetings, watching my eyes so I never looked wrong at the wrong dude and dissed him to my own fatality. I drew the line at drugs and drink and shoplifting as did most of my fellow hoops students, despite the stereotypes they bear—and I picked up as much of what passed among almost-teens for street cool as I could.

On the court, however, I was all business. Hockey had made me a good athlete; I should say hockey and my grandfather, because of course it was he who year after year was whispering strategy and strength and style in my ear as soon as I stepped off the ice. The night before I left for basketball camp he said one very interesting thing to me. It was the closest he came to putting basketball in its place behind *"le grand jeu"* (a restraint that probably kept him up nights muttering to himself in the mirror). He said, "Notice if in this basketball sport the coaches compliment the players for—what is it called?—*hustle*. Notice that. Listen, and see if you hear the words 'Good hustle, Jim!' or 'That is the way to hustle, Tom!' "

I was counting my rap audiotapes or something and barely heard him. "Why?" I said.

He patted my back. "Just see," he said. "See if 'hustle' is something *extra* in this game, something for which one is given special praise."

Well, of course, the first time someone ran hard after a ball bouncing out of bounds and dove into the folding chairs, every coach in the place hollered praise for his hustle. And the first time a guard who had coughed up the ball ran back and almost caught the kid who stole it from him and took it in for a layup, they clapped for his hustle. And the time . . .

My grandfather never had to explain his point.

In basketball, you get extra credit for "going all out" every once in a while, and the effort is rare enough that it *shows*—"Wow, that's *hustle*." Hockey, I realized then and realize more every day, puts basketball and its special bits of "hustle" to shame. In hockey, you hit the ice going all out and you don't slow down or let a possible play pass you by for as long as you are out there, stabbing at the puck in the corners with guys giving you shots to the kidneys, racing faster than you thought you could skate just to beat an icing touch-up, muscling a bigger player six inches to the left so his shooting angle at the goal won't be as dangerous if he should ever get the puck. There is no moderation, no selection of *this* play to try and *that* one to let go. Then your shift is over and you drag yourself back to the bench covered with sweat and sometimes a little blood, and the guys waiting to go out and pick up where you left off see you and swear *they* aren't going to look any better when *their* shift is over. . . .

So I hit the hardwood running, used to it. I had more stamina than anyone else, and more of what looked like Desire (a basketball coach's favorite concept) but really was just concentration under pressure. Of course, I lacked skills. But it didn't take me long to dribble pretty well. And though I never managed the art of shooting I did master the easier means of propelling passes wherever I wanted.

And I wanted to propel them to lots of interesting places. *That* is why I looked like such an ace: I "saw the whole floor" as they say in hoops, I "read the play," I seemed to compute the relative speeds and positions of the nine other bodies out there, and get the ball to exactly the right person in exactly the right place, even when he himself had not foreseen being there.

How did I do it? I never told anyone, I let it seem I had just been blessed with a profound wisdom about how offense worked. But it is a fact that once you have been a playmaker in a sport where everyone moves twenty-five miles per hour and can swivel and reverse and spin on his feet without the slightest drag of friction, well, running in sticky-rubber sneakers on a wooden floor seems like watching a movie in slow-motion.

By the end of the first week of camp I was the new hotshot, the one people from other scrimmages stopped and came over to watch. It made me quite the cool one off the court; I recall that when my grandfather visited my dormitory that first weekend, my room was full of rude kids and I did not even remove my blaring yellow earplugs to speak with him.

He left without saying much, but he returned for graduation night, when an all-star team selected from us campers played a group of Georgetown freshmen in town for early workouts. They killed us as a team, of course, but they didn't kill *me*—I personally shredded their defense for thirty-one assists and was the unanimous MVP for the camp. The only reason my team scored at *all* was that I kept surprising them with the ball in a position from which they couldn't help but put it in. I even scored one layup as well. It was a loss, but for me it was a triumph.

But—as my wise grandfather must have foreseen, but never alluded to—it was a hollow triumph, and a quick one too. I could pass a basketball—so what? I didn't really *like* passing a basketball—it's just that I proved I *could*. Playing the game during the rest of the summer was nothing but a drag. Running in sneakers made my feet hot. Not being able to spin and slide made me feel clumsy and earthbound. Playing a game in which someone scored almost every time his team had the ball seemed melodramatic compared with the gritty difficulty of even getting a *shot* off in hockey. And size! The fact that somebody could dominate a basketball game because he had the genes to make him tall—well, I rebelled against it. Big hockey players had certain advantages, but they were short certain skills too. Our team's best player was its smallest.

On the whole, my triumph—both in my head and on the courts where I let some of my new friends coax me into a few pickup games at first— faded fast, and I found myself longing for the first day I could lace up my skates and start to *move*.

The wind whips some dust in my face. I turn and look at Marshall, who squints behind his glasses. Marshall. Marshall did not attend the Georgetown camp—it was very expensive, I remember, with another pang of guilt—but he accompanied my grandfather to the graduation game.

What did he think? Did he imagine himself on the receiving end of those thirty-one brilliant passes, and thousands more all the way to the NBA? If so, he has never said a word to me about it.

Marshall and I became friends soon after I moved here from Baltimore. We met each other at a little loop off the Severn River where, we had both separately discovered, water sliders congregated to sun themselves on a particular sycamore branch that angled out of the black shallow water. The first time I saw him I had been crouched for perhaps fifteen minutes thinking I was alone, watching the turtles crane their necks, pull them in, skitter off with a *plup* into the pool. Suddenly a voice that was not nearly as alarming as it should have been, given my belief that I was by myself, said, "I wonder if I come here because that water is the exact color of my skin."

I had located him within seconds, straddling a medium-high limb up in a living sycamore, both spidery hands out in front of him encircling the splotchy bark. I checked; it was true, the water *did* match his skin.

"I guess *I* ought to bring a Yoo-Hoo with me tomorrow, then," I said.

He laughed. "You aren't Yoo-Hoo colored.

That's not a color that can be found anywhere outside a laboratory in New Jersey."

"Maybe I was made in a lab in Jersey."

"No," he said, "you're from Baltimore, originally from Montreal, and you speak French. And your color, I have decided, is pine bark." The way he said it made me feel he had been giving it some thought for some time. I realized I was in the presence of a watcher. It takes one to know one.

So from that point on, we Watched together. It was a peculiar kind of friendship, because the things we *did*—as opposed to *watched*—were very different. I was a singer, a show-off with a mouth, performing anywhere six people and a microphone could be found; Marshall was the quietest person in the school. I was smart enough, but not in ways that school ever seemed to reach out for; Marshall attacked every new subject and mastered his textbooks by October, and starting in the fourth grade was taking a taxi every afternoon to the high school to study trigonometry and calculus and physics and three foreign languages.

And of course, I played ice hockey, while Marshall became a basketball star.

As early as the third grade Marshall showed signs that he was going to be very tall, and this meant he became the first-chosen every day on the small courts everyone crowded at recess. But it was as if he were determined *not* to use the gift of height, and he played terribly as a center. Rebounds slid through his hands, passes bounced at his feet and off his shins and out of bounds. He set no picks. He didn't jump. A few times, as if suddenly taken crazy, he would snatch the ball and dribble *away* from the basket, until he was beyond everyone, and then he would laugh and juke and twirl around—"playing little," he called it—finally dribbling back through the defense to the corner and pulling up for a jumper.

Later, when the Marshall legend was well-known to us all, we realized what we should have recognized back then: that he was playing every day at the *high* school, where he was no longer the Tall Kid, and where he learned to do all of the things that now make him such an amazing player *and* the Tall Kid to boot.

But he was always alone out there. He made nice passes and thanked his teammates for theirs, but he played by himself. Once after a JV game in which he scored 50 of his teams 55 points, got about 25 rebounds, blocked more than a dozen shots, and committed no fouls or turnovers, I asked him if he thought it was possible to have a perfect game. He looked me straight in the eye and said, quite seriously, "Certainly. The ball has a perfect game *every* game."

As Marshall got closer to middle school and Coach Kantuu, it became clear that all he would need to go wherever a ballplayer could hope to go was—a great playmaker, a passer, a Cousy to his Russell, a Magic to his Jabbar, a Stockton to his Malone. For Coach Kantuu, this was an especially frustrating problem, because he had been an ace playmaker himself, twice leading the ACC in assists; why couldn't he find the kid Marshall needed?

Then I showed my stuff at Georgetown. In front of Marshall, with Coach Kantuu sitting right beside him. There he was—the Playmaker! And he went to the right school! And—most wondrous of all— he happened also to be Marshall's only buddy!

Word got around fast, faster than I could de-cline the honors being prematurely bestowed on me. Coach Kantuu, I am sure, was the main gossip. But as I failed to play in all those pickup games eagerly awaiting me, as I failed to come to early JV camp, and finally as I failed to promise I would come out for basketball at all, the truth leaked back against the flow of the praise: Dude is giving it all *up*, turning his back on his main *brother*, turning his back on all of *us* in fact, just so he can go play some jive sport his foreign *grandaddy* likes, a sport in which, as one nasty wit put it, "he got to let a bunch of white boys chase him around with sticks!"

So, as we walk home in the wind, I can't be cross with Marshall for speaking the truth. My flirtation with hoops was nothing but my moment of rebelling against my good old male authority figure, my noble wise grandfather, a pretty ill-chosen adversary, actually—sadly isolated far from his city, his language, his music, his coffee, his bread—with only his grandson to give him a small grip on his cold, difficult, low-scoring, complicated sport.

And I knew very well that Marshall, alone, understood it all.

Like me, Marshall doesn't seem to belong to

any of the hip elements of *blackness* in school and the life that extends from it. But he does play basketball. Basketball is inside the circle. Hockey is not. It doesn't matter that Marshall sees his basketball as having nothing to do with his ethnicity— "What, if I were a Vietno-Mexican, you wouldn't like my 32 a game?" he once snapped at an overzealous fan who was using me—the faithful sidekick—as an example of "not fulfilling your thing as a Brother." The fact is, the man plays the right game. I could not have chosen a less right one if that had been my goal. As one hipster said, to my undying amusement, during one of the mild debates that used to take place about whether or not I deserved to be admitted to the human race, "What, hockey? It's white to white in white *on* white. Check out the ice, baby. That your idea of color?"

My musical abilities seemed to offer me a way to make the jump to my school's acceptably-black culture. But at first, during the first years I was going public as a singer, I let too many, well, *white* music teachers talk me into singing (very white) show tunes at assemblies. Later, when I got to middle school last year, I pushed the (black) jazz teacher to form a "combo" and then pushed to basically turn it into a small swing band. Not swing as in (white) Glenn Miller, all smooth major-chords and middle-ground rhythms, but swing as in (black) early Duke Ellington, hot from the jungle, with bwah-mutes and growly trombones and angular piano playing against an aggressive plucked bass—over all of which, in and out of all of which, I would sneak and slither in my smoothness, singing (black) songs that may have become (white) standards, but which never lost their spell or their sinew. Alas, that kind of music is very difficult, to teach, and to play. It was much easier for our "jazz" combo to lapse into a Weather Report–like niceness that had a hint of The Islands and a hint of Soul and a hint of Europe—all of it boring, dreadful, as unhip as could be, sounding ten-years-further-past with each song. Not even the *adults* at our single concert liked the music. I was delighted when the band I had pushed into existence fell apart after one season.

Strangely enough, the hockey team came together for one crazy-wild, incredibly loud, totally improvised, fabulously emotional concert—but we had never tried it again as yet, and anyway, it was too peculiar to pass with the Yo boys.

Then suddenly one day I recognized the shy, quiet guy with the large eyes always turned on his text that I sat next to in French class—he was none other than DJ Fook, the hippest, coolest trip-hop mixmaster going, the pride of the cultural coalition that called itself the "darkside" of the school. He was the only kid with a regular mixing gig in a Baltimore club, where on one of the non high-crowd nights he sliced and diced samples and songs and threw in an occasional mumbled rap while a drum machine gave the clientele something to dance to.

So when I recognized him I was searching for just the right compliment, when, to my surprise he half-turned his head toward me, glancing away from his text and at the floor halfway between our desks, which served as deep eye-contact for Fook, and said, to my surprise, "Um, like, I really like your voice, man. Your voice is, like, the mellowest thing."

I was too stupefied to say much beyond thanks. I guess it was a compliment—"mellow" was not exactly a big trip-hop adjective. But Fook made it clear: "If you want to know, man, sometimes I feel, like, I mean, I just need *just* that sound, you know? I mean, I do a sample, something harsh, man, some bad drop of acid on your ear, okay? and the thing I need is, just"—and here he half-closed his eyes and extended his thin lips so far out in a hollow pucker that he looked like some kind of exotic flower—"HOOOOOOOoooooo. . . . ." Then he blushed (yes, black people blush), and said in swallowed words something about maybe getting a sample or something. . . .

I had made a point of following up Fook's opening—I suggested we get together, me singing vocalise over his stuff, me singing words or even rapping over it, me standing offstage and throwing in the occasional "HOOOOOoooo" at a secret signal from him. As with Marshall, the thing was, I really liked Fook. But Fook was a careful dude. He was the only kid with a real-life gig and he actually did not want to share any part of it. It turns out he talked about the two of us doing something together while I was making all of my offers to do this or that, but all he wanted from me was a few taped samples of my voice, for use in his mixes. He neglected to tell his fans the limits on our work relationship were *his* idea, not that snooty Hoke's, so kids assumed I was the reluctant one. I was disappointed, to tell the truth. I had begun to see some interesting possibilities, using my voice for textures and roles inside a song I hadn't imagined before. Maybe Fook was smart to get my samples and cut me out early; I would have been a pushy partner.

During the few weeks I was doing my thing with Fook I was actually okay with my darkside brethren. With my grandfather however, I seemed a horrible stupidity. Not only was I throwing my voice away on something that certainly did not deserve that ultimate word of honor, Song, but I was a traitor to the years of tutelage during which he had taught me not just the music and lyrics to all of those great tunes, but had helped me find my way to all kinds of personal nuance in phrasing, rhythm, play with the beat, scat, everything. He happened to come upon me in the living room one day when I was listening to a heavily "harshed" loop Fook had made of me singing a phrase from

Billy Strayhorn's "Lush Life," my grandfather's life-long favorite song.

My grandfather did not change *his* mind as quickly as Fook's fans did when it was perceived that I somehow considered myself too good to work with him. They turned on me in two beats. And it took months after that to convince him that I had not "sucked him dry" of music so I could turn it into "trashes." (The French plural is much worse than the English singular.) But I did convince him, though perhaps I never made it all the way back into his absolute favor; I kept singing, by myself and, at my undeniably earnest request, with him; I kept getting better, which meant I kept loving the music more and more; I made no more ventures into hipper types of hoppin.' But—as much as I loved "Stardust"—I could not quite forget some of those possibilities I had foreseen before the Fook used me and cast me away. I made my grandfather no promises. So, perhaps, with reason, he never completely trusted me again.

But there was always hockey. . . .

For some reason our defensemen cannot handle the puck tonight. During the first shift of the game Dooby flubs an outlet pass from beside the cage and the puck dribbles up the slot so that a forechecking center can whip it past Zip unseen. Two shifts later Woodsie has wound up and is zooming through everyone with his beautiful grace, but the puck rolls off his stick at the red line and he doesn't notice. He keeps skating and faking, and all the rest of us do too, but meanwhile our opponents have picked up the puck and gone in on poor Zip, three on zero, scoring easily. Near the end of the first period Barry catches a high centering pass in his glove, drops it to the ice near his stick blade, and watches, frozen in horror, as he fans on it and leaves it sitting on edge for their center, who is *on his chest*, to sweep in.

Offensively we are not much better. I fall into a bad habit I would recognize all by myself even if

I did not have my grandfather to harass me about it whenever it occurs: I carry the puck too long, and then have to make *perfect* daring thread-the-needle passes, most of which don't get through, when I could have gotten the puck to the man more easily if I had let it go a second earlier. Unfortunately, the later pass *looks* more creative and daring, and thus causes fans to think more highly of me when in fact I ought to be subjected to a little scorn. My grandfather always accuses me (wrongfully, and he knows it deep down) of doing this on purpose when I am feeling cranky at not scoring goals, and because I'm vain.

Still, some things are dependable even when all else seems to crack apart. Boot has a hat trick by the second period and we are only down two goals halfway through the third when Cody intercepts a pass along the blue line between the defensemen on their power play, and blindly backhands the puck along the ice past the skates of the goalie, who was busy scraping snow out of his crease. A freakier play we'll never see.

A ripple goes through the bench. Freaky or not, now we want it.

Boot asks the coach to double-shift him, which the coach never does, and this time I hope he holds to his rule: I can tell Boot is tired, even though his adrenaline keeps flashing the number 4! in front of his eyes. Instead, with two minutes left, Coach sends out the line that was supposed to take the ice—tonight's version of the Spaz Line, featuring Shark, Java, and Feets as the the Spazzes, Ernie as the mildly adequate non-Spaz Regular, and Billy as the Wild Card. This is how the Spaz Line is always configured: three true Spazzes, one okay Regular, and one Wild Card, meaning a player (Shinny is another frequent WC) who has very streaky talents that can be superior taken one by one, but which are deployed in harmony only if we get very, very lucky.

Billy is a great puzzle to us all. He is the prettiest skater on the team, yet he never had a lesson, or a pair of in-line street skates, or so much as a pre-tryout drill. He is not as fast as Cody but he can maneuver through any obstacle course of hostile bodies wielding sticks. In his offensive zone he takes your breath away, wheeling in tight circles where most people could barely swerve, creating ice for himself where there seemed to be no room for him to move or stickhandle or gather speed, which he does with uncanny suddenness. His shot is always hard and low and dead on net, even from a terrible angle; once he scored a goal from the corner, straddling the goal line, with the goalie holding the post against him. I still don't know how the puck got through, but Billy put it through.

Yet Billy can also forget everything he ought to know about the *game* of hockey. He skates offsides far more than any other player on the team, including all the Spazzes put together. And for all of his skating grace with the puck, he is a lazy plodder without it, never moving his feet when checking a puck carrier side-by-side, using his arms and stick to hold the player back as he pulls away. In the defensive zone he chases the puck, wearing him-self out and, at the same time, leaving his man totally open. Perhaps strangest of all, the same great hands, that let him stickhandle and shoot with such precision and strength, turn to stone when he gets the puck in a defensive position: he panics, and swats at it as if it were a rat and he held a broom. Yet some nights . . .

All of us on the bench are watching to see which way Billy will bounce.

Against all odds, Shark wins the face-off, and Ernie, looking amused and mildly interested, rockets an excellent dump over everyone's head to the far corner, toward which the opposing right defenseman—a tall, smart player who is the team's captain—races furiously against Billy for the prize.

We are all leaning forward, lunging with Billy as if we were watching a sprint in the Olympics. The defenseman has a better angle but has to do a little skip step to approach perfectly; Billy smoothly crosses over instead, and picks up half a step.

"I'd trade my exquisite cleft chin for that crossover of his," says Dooby.

"You don't have a cleft chin," says Shinny.

Dooby looks startled and feels his face. "That's right—I already swapped it for Woodsie's backhand pass."

It is clear now that Billy is going to beat the other kid to the puck. As if he refuses to lose the race, the defenseman hunkers lower and pushes through two huge driving strides, straight at the puck, which lies a foot from the dasher and boards.

Billy, two feet from the puck, suddenly pulls up with a huge spray.

The defenseman, realizing he has skated too hard too late, tries to swerve with one skate and stop with the other, succeeding only in crashing in an ugly sprawl against the boards and ice.

Billy meanwhile has pulled the puck back, allowing all of the other opponents who were caught up in their captain's charge to skate through the circle and by him. He cuts back toward the slot behind them, and, using one flailing winger as a screen, fires a low shot that zips just inside the near post.

The bench explodes. The opposing captain slowly climbs to his skates and heads for the gate at the corner, apparently injured. Billy is so excited, and skating so well, that no one can catch him to rub his helmet.

"Change," says the coach.

But somehow Billy doesn't get the message, and no one thinks to count heads, and when the puck is dropped Billy is still out there: we have too many men on the ice. It's a bench minor, and we will have to play the last 1:01 shorthanded. The other team takes new life.

As soon as his center wins the face-off, the

opposing coach pulls his goalie. Now it is six on four—Cody, Dooby, Woodsie, and me.

They have obviously practiced their game with the extra man, because they skate in onside and set up perfectly around the perimeter, with a man on the half boards and another cruising between the slot and the space behind the net. We are all side skating with our sticks stretched out, trying to hold our box, hoping they will get impatient and take a long shot Zip can see all the way, giving us a crack at the rebound. . . .

"Good work guys, only ten more seconds," Dooby gasps loudly to me. The winger with the puck hears him, and his eyes go wide, and he winds up for a slapshot from fifty feet. Dooby drops to the ice at the perfect moment to block the shot with his kneepads, *thwock*, I pick the puck away from his legs and push it up to Woodsie, who is racing for the empty net with the whole opposing team in chase—but then he doubles neatly back toward the boards and skates calmly back into our defensive zone, leaving the enemy up-ice. I look up at the clock: :15, :14, :13 . . . What?

"So I lied," says Dooby.

As the first attacker crosses the blue line, with :09 on the clock, Woodsie lofts a high, soft forehand that lands just short of their blue line and saucers slowly into the corner. We are shorthanded, so there is no icing.

The buzzer sounds. Dooby gets the game puck, probably the first one ever given entirely for work with the mouth.

After we all got dressed, Barry and Woodsie and Shinny and I dump our bags by the bleachers and go off to the nine-foot air hockey tournament. I always win. This time I don't.

It should have tipped me off to something. Later, at home, when I unpack my equipment to air it out, I find that someone has stolen my skates. Not just stolen them, though: replaced them. For in the end pocket where I keep my Bauers is a pair of slightly worn hightop leather basketball shoes. It only takes me about thirty seconds to recognize them as the ones I wore only once, for two weeks, while I was an ace playmaker African-American stereotype of destiny. I put them away shortly after, and hadn't thought about them, or intended ever to wear them, ever again.

ithout your skates you can't even think about playing hockey. *Your* skates, not someone else's, not some new ones from the store. Other pieces of equipment you can borrow or buy in an emergency—shoulder pads, elbow pads, knee pads, gloves, pants, even a helmet. But your whole game comes from the ice up, and the way you connect to that ice through that blade depends on how close you feel to it. That closeness is something you develop by *living* in your skates, hour after hour after hour. Somebody knew what he was doing when he snatched mine. He knew where to hurt me.

I didn't tell my grandfather about the missing skates. I didn't think I needed to, even though we had another game two days after the game at which they were stolen. I had a feeling I would be hearing about them, and I had a feeling that one way or another it would be possible for me to get them back.

It was almost bedtime and I was just finishing my math homework when my grandfather came to the door of my room, wearing his maroon silk dressing gown, and, with a frown of curiosity, told me I was wanted on the telephone.

"Marshall?" I asked as I put my pencil down and stood up.

He said nothing so I looked. He was studying me. He looked a little more skeptical than I had seen him look since the time I ignored Cody open at the post three times in one shift and shot all three times myself (I did not score). As I slid by him I smelled his shaving soap. He always shaves before bed, with sandalwood shaving soap and a badger brush and a safety razor.

"Are you singing somewhere?" he asked me.

I looked at him, surprised. "Singing? What do you mean? I sing all the time—"

He shook his head and waved my answer away. He looked at me again, then shook his head some more, and without another word walked down the hall and closed the door to his room. I stood for a second, then went down to his music study to take the call.

I could hear the telephone from the doorway, and now I had an idea what my grandfather was wondering about. From the earpiece came a brash clanging that was cut every couple of seconds with a synthesized drumbeat that sheared the music off while it lasted. Good old hip-hop; my grandfather and I used to argue about my interest in it every day. When he asked if I were singing, I should have heard quotation marks around the word "singing"—he was asking if I had joined a hop crew.

As I crossed the study I would not have been surprised to see the phone headset hopping on the table where it rested. When I picked it up I said, "Okay, cut it down," and the volume dropped immediately.

A voice said, "Just wanted to get your attention, yours and the old dude's."

"He's my grandfather," I said, "not 'the old dude.' Who are you?"

"The guy who told the kids who took your skates not to take your skates," the voice said.

I had not expected a lot of things I heard in this voice. First of all, I had of course assumed my skates had been snatched by some angry Yo kids looking either simply to mess me up or to hold my skates ransom until I promised to play basketball for Coach Kantuu. For a few minutes I had even suspected *him* of setting up the theft, but I dismissed that idea. He was a fanatic, and like all fanatics he was sly and manipulative, but ultimately I thought he was honest. This voice sounded honest, too. And it was no Yo kid. If you are a singer you become a student of voices, and whenever you hear a person speak you are aware of a hundred little things that tell you about the speaker—consonants dropped or slurred or over-defined, vowels stretched or clipped, all kinds of stuff. Right away I knew I was speaking with someone at least a few years older than me and my middle-school friends, someone intelligent, someone with a lot of confidence, and someone with some kind of power. Also, someone with a loud hi-fi.

As if he were reading my thoughts, he said, "How'd you like that thing I was playing?"

"I don't know," I said. "It was so loud I couldn't hear it."

He laughed. "A little thing I just put together on

an eight-track with two samplers using, among other things, a few bars from two of the Brandenburg Concerti—not the harpsichord parts, I hate harpsichords—and a loop of the man then called Cassius Clay—"

"'Float like a butterfly,'" I said, "'sting like a bee.'"

"That's the man. Actually, I was using a sample of the phrase he used to refer to Sonny Liston as a big ugly bear. The man had a way with the word 'ugly.'"

"Didn't he also used to refer to himself as 'pretty'? I remember something about 'my body, my face. . . .'"

"Right memory, wrong word. Clay called himself 'beautiful.' It was Little Richard who was always telling us how 'pretty' he was."

"I guess he is, if you like that kind of pretty."

"Which I do not, although 'Lucille' is Number Eight in my personal pantheon of Top Tunes. But I did not call you up at this late hour to discuss pretty Little Richard."

"Let me warn you right now," I said. "If you or the people who took my skates intend to use them to pressure me into trying out for the basketball team tomorrow, you or they had better be careful not to say so."

"Very good. As it happens, I am not linked with the thieves who did your footwear. I cannot claim to know what use they plan to make of their booty. Not my thing, know what I'm sayin'? In fact, basketball is not my thing. I have absolutely no stake, nor even any interest, in whether or not you decide to have anything to do with Clark Weatherspoon or the young men he has enslaved to his vicarious ambitions, notwithstanding your friend Marshall, who is perfectly equipped to take care of himself even in World War III. Do you understand me?"

"All right. Yes."

"Then we need not refer again to this basketball business."

"Do you have my skates?"

"Let's say that I have purchased an option on your skates—with the idea of restoring them to you—and can readily exercise that option and get them to you immediately."

"Tell me what you want."

He hesitated. "My vanity is irresistible. Why am I different from skate-kidnappers?"

"I suspect you are not crude."

"Ah. All right. Well, then let's get to it. I want you to sing."

"To sing?"

"I'll explain: I am a promoter. My business is, specifically, live music, in the more artistically adventurous African-American clubs in the Baltimore-Washington-Annapolis area. But I am also a tinkerer. I have a gift that applies to weird machines and technology nobody has even thought of yet. Whereas you have the most beautiful voice that I have ever heard."

"You haven't heard my grandfather."

"Begging your pardon, I have heard the great Jean-Lucien. With all due respect, I like your prospects better."

"Because I'm younger?"

"Yes, partly because of that—but not just because you may be supposed to live longer, as you may choke on a chicken bone a half hour from now, Lord forbid. Your youth recommends you for another reason."

"I'm more likely to get into something avant-garde?"

"Possibly, though I wouldn't put it past Jean-

Lucien to recognize any progressive movement that was of genuine artistic merit. Then again, I may be romanticizing; he could just as easily be conservative beyond belief."

"You are. He is. *Especially* about music. The last acceptable innovation was the plunger-mute."

"Anyway, I'm onto something else."

I thought. "My pre-pubescent falsetto?"

He laughed. "No, I trust your falsetto will grow along with you, hormones and all." He paused for a moment. "What I am thinking of is something you're probably going to deny, something you may not even admit to yourself. See, what I am thinking of appealing to is this: your deep, troublesome, discomfiting, secret discontent, completely original but completely universal, at failing to belong, to feel you are a part of the common culture of the people and times that surround you. To feel like one of the guys."

I said nothing.

"Let's face it," he said. "It's hard for someone like you—someone with his own style and taste. You'd like to fit in, somewhere, with black teenage life in America. But you don't want to have to play basketball to do it, or wear tacky earphones every-where you go *blasting* the sound of very cheap drum machines." He paused. "Still," he said softly, "you want to get inside the tent."

I waited for a minute, placing my hands on the cover over the keys of my grandfather's piano. When I started to speak I had to clear my throat.

"So I do some singing for you through your hardware and next thing you know I'm hip? Instead of cast out of the tribe with my spear broken, I go 'shooby shooby shooby' into your MacIntosh in the right club and my brothers and sisters change my nickname from Hokey to Rastaman? It's that simple?"

"It could be. It just could be."

"Hm." I thought about it. Two years before I had flirted with some hip-hop stuff, even sat at an open mike a couple of times at a "pre-teen" club in a church basement where somebody's older brother imitated a drum machine on a real snare drum and another kid played fuzz-bass and the minister did his part by broadcasting a loop of Sly and the Family Stone's "Everyday People" played backwards, over and over and over on the tinny little P.A. It was actually kind of surreal and cool, all of us making up awkward raps to the same all-men-are-brothers song played backwards for three hours.

"Will you tell me what it will be like?"

"No. Partly because that depends on you. What you bring to the performance is the great factor of chance, uncertainty, improvisation."

"That's only 'partly.' You wouldn't tell me also for other reasons."

"That is correct."

"Such as that I might think it sounds foolish? Or impossible? Or dangerous?"

He said nothing.

"When is this gig?" I asked.

"Tomorrow night."

"Ah. After basketball tryouts."

"Who cares about basketball tryouts?"

"Right." I thought. "You said a club. It's in a club, one of the hip-trip places?"

"I only work on the cutting edge, friend."

"How am I supposed to be allowed inside? I don't look close to the age when I could even *fake* an ID—"

"Please," he said. "Don't insult me. I take care

of my performers at no risk to themselves."

"Speaking of taking care of your—"

"You would perform for approximately twenty minutes, during which time I can guarantee that your audience will include such leaders of the community as to spread word of your success to their worshipful followers within an hour. *Plus* you will receive five hundred dollars."

"I will receive five hundred dollars," I said, "*plus* my ice skates."

As if consulting his watch, he pulled back from the mouthpiece a little and said, "It is now . . . 11:51. You have already received your ice skates."

I put the phone down. As I went through the hall I saw through the little windows in the top of the front door that the porch light was out. I opened the door and felt the bulb. It was warm. I screwed it three-quarters of a turn, and it came on. Its light revealed a cardboard box on the doormat. I took the box inside, closed the door, and carried the box back to the study. With the phone wedged against my ear I opened the box and unwrapped the two packages of butcher paper inside.

"Yours?" said the voice.

"Mine," I said. "You exercise your options fast. Either that, or you knew I was going to say yes."

"I chose a business I love," he said, "so that I would have to ask only those questions people *wanted* to answer that way. I will send a car for you tomorrow at 10 p.m. If you like, by all means invite Jean-Lucien."

"He'll be asleep."

"Not if he knows you are going to be singing somewhere."

eight

oach Kantuu looked nervous even though all he was doing was giving out the page numbers for homework to his last-period math class. He looked nervous, as if he were thinking ahead to the basketball tryouts just thirty-two minutes away, nervous even though he already knew exactly who was coming because he let it be known through the school that unless he invited you, you needn't show up; and if he *did* invite you, you had pretty much made the team.

Just as the bell rang and the kids in his class bolted to their feet, he ran his hand through his hair and looked up at the clock, and that is when he saw me.

His face went into this blankness of confusion, and I realized that at just that moment he did not know who I was. For a flash I felt like taking advantage of this and bolting along with the last few Algebra I stragglers, but I didn't, and anyway he only took two seconds to get it. He didn't even say hello.

"You're trying out," he said.

"Sorry to barge in and take up your time," I said, "but I don't know the drill, and everybody else—"

"It's fine, it's cool," he said, reaching out both hands for my arms as if I were going to vanish. He looked me in the eyes, surprised and happy at first, then, after only a couple of seconds, crafty and doubtful and suspicious.

I didn't let him ask. "I just decided to give it a try," I said. "All on my own. Nobody kidnapped my dog, nobody is holding Marshall in a cave with a gun to his head. I *do* have to admit that flattery has a lot to do with it. I mean, having people talk about you like you're Penny Hardaway just because you get lucky at one summer camp—"

"We'll take the State four years running," he said. His eyes weren't suspicious anymore; they were arrogant now. " 'Lucky at one summer camp'?" He took one hand off my arm and pointed at his own eyes. "I was there, remember? I *saw*. And I am not easy to trick with 'luck,' boy. What I *saw* was what I *had*—*you* have it now, and you couldn't hide it if you tried, and nobody knows better than I do how deep it goes, how far it will take your team. It's us, we're the ones who make the game *go*, we are the playmakers." He was grinning now, and he threw his head back and crowed.

"Coach," I said, "remember, I only played basketball that one time in my life—"

But he wasn't listening. Mumbling to himself with lots of "Yesss!" and such stuff sounding through, he quickly closed up his classroom and hustled me out and down the stairs and through the halls to the gymnasium. For the last ten minutes he talked over every player on the team except Marshall, telling me how each kid was *almost* a complete player, each one had this or that set of skills, but this one lacked a step of that essential lateral quickness, you know?, or that one just didn't have the soft hands for turning the hard pass into the lofted shot. I just nodded and let him run on. We passed a few groups of black kids hanging at their lockers, some Yo kids and some jocks, and all of them said "Hey! Kantuu!," but he was so busy chattering that he didn't even wave. Then we got to the gym, and he stopped before the double doors.

"Okay," I said, starting to move off toward the locker room. "I guess I'll see you—"

"Let me ask you something," he said, fixing me with a heavy stare.

I had one hand on the push-doors. "Sure," I said. "What is it?"

He stared at me for another minute, then without saying anything he beckoned to me, and turned to go through the single door twenty feet away that said COACH on it in white letters. He unlocked it quickly with a key, held it open behind him with one arm without turning to look at me, then pointed at a chair near his desk. There were photos in frames on the wall and certificates and stuff, and a fat frame with his red MARYLAND jersey spread out behind the glass, number 11, and a couple of trophies that looked pretty dark and old. I didn't get to look at anything very closely, though, because he had pulled open a couple of drawers behind his desk and, saying "A-ha!," pulled out a flat wooden rectangle with a lot of inch-wide pieces of brass lined up in columns on it. He held it out to me, and nodded. I took it.

Across the top it said MARYLAND SCHOOLBOY MARKS AAA. I read a couple of the little brass pieces and realized what this was: a plaque listing all of the state records in the various individual categories, with the record-holder's name and the year he set his mark. I knew what to look for, and in no time I found the 'assist' categories, and read that he had two: ASSISTS, SINGLE SEASON and ASSISTS, CAREER. (The only one he didn't get was ASSISTS, GAME, which I couldn't help noticing was 22, considerably less than that famous 31 figure. . . .

"Wow," I said, handing the plaque back to him. "Congratulations. I mean, I knew you were like—"

"Wipe me right off," he said.

"Excuse me?"

"Take these tired old pieces of brass right *off* this record plaque." He tossed it carelessly behind him. It landed on a pile of old newspapers and made the whole thing slide into a corner. "Make it look like C. WEATHERSPOON was nothing but a footnote, not the best playmaker the state ever saw. Wipe me *out*, Maestro, with those over-the-shoulder drop passes to the trailer on the break and those baseball throws court-length right off the dribble and those perfectly arched, just-out-of-the-defender's-reach lobs. Marshall's got to be drooling over *them*."

"Actually, he doesn't even know I'm here."

He gaped at me. "What do you mean?"

"I told you, I came on my own. But let me remind you again, Coach, my just showing up doesn't mean—"

"You mean this is going to be a *surprise*? For *everybody*?"

I fidgeted. "Well, I guess, but it's not exactly big news or anything, I'm just—"

He crowed again. Then he came over and stood me up and bustled me out the door, with this smug smile on his face the whole time. "You know where the locker room is," he said. "Go get changed and start shooting some free throws."

"Okay," I said, moving toward the double doors.

"A *surprise!*" I heard him say behind me, as his door slammed shut on a kind of cackling laugh.

nine

Because the coach had kept me for so long, I was the last guy to come into the locker room. In the second before everyone turned to see who it was, the room was like one of those old cartoons in which two guys are having a wild fight, with smoke and lightning bolts and dust and chickens and cats and twelve or thirteen arms and legs apiece poking in and out all over the place, and you always know no one is getting hurt, it's just funny.

But when they turned and saw me they stopped snapping towels at each other or playing keep away with a sneaker or putting jockstraps on their head. They looked at me, and they looked serious—like they could not decide whether to eat me or bury me.

"Hi," I said with a bright smile. Going for the humorous. "Nice to see you dudes!"

No one smiled. One very muscular short guy— obviously a guard, just stared at my eyes the whole time I changed, beaming black hate death-rays and making sure I knew it. When we went out to shoot around he made sure he was always at my elbow, staring. If I picked up a ball bouncing by, to shoot it, he slapped it hard out of my hands without taking his eyes off my face, and said, "That my ball. You don't *touch* my ball." He never bothered to shoot with one of the balls either. I got the message.

The other players were not exactly warm to me, but they had all heard about my camp experience, and probably they had all been among those who put me down behind my back for being a traitor to my race, and most of all they were willing to accept *anyone* who could help them win more, so they were moderately cool. Marshall, who had already been on the floor swishing left-handed hook after left-handed hook while the rest of us dressed, nodded at me once distractedly, but that was all.

Coach was a little late coming out, which gave me a chance to look up at the bleachers. I was very surprised to see about three times the usual crowd. A forward named Perrone saw me looking and came over to stand beside me. He nodded at the people getting settled to watch practice. "Part of it's tryouts," he said. "But mostly they here to see can you play."

"I don't think so," I said. "I just told Coach myself."

He looked at me. "How long ago?"

I thought. "A half an hour."

He laughed. "A half hour *plenty*. Man, ain't you never heard of the *drum*?"

I laughed too. I guessed that some of the groups we had passed in the hall got the word around. Now, I don't mind crowds for hockey games, because I know I can *play* hockey. I was a little less eager to show off my unknown basketball skills.

A whistle blew, and everyone ran to midcourt and dropped to his knees. Coach was standing in the middle, ignoring us, looking at some things on a clipboard. After a while he said, "Marshall, how many we got?"

"Fifteen," Marshall said.

"Fourteen," whispered the kid who hung around my cerebellum.

Coach finished jotting something and looked up at us. "Right," he said. "Most of you know this is not the usual kind of tryouts, where a huge number of mediocre players waste our time showing they can't play and make me cut them so they go home and cry. Almost all of you have been played for me before, and everyone but Hokey here"—he pointed to me and I nodded—"has been in here working out for two weeks. This is not so much a tryout as our first official unofficial practice. Even so, we need to see what people can do, so instead of running drills all day, we'll spend most of the time in a full-length, full-court scrimmage, with clock and scorekeeper."

"And humiliation," said my shadow.

"Very likely," I said.

"One word. I do not believe in special favors. You all know that Hokey showed some righteous stuff as a point guard at Georgetown summer camp, and you know I and many of you have been trying to recruit him to come out for the team. But this is as far as his recruitment goes: From here on out, he lives or dies by what he does on *this* floor, not on his rep. Any questions?"

One kid, probably a large guard, raised his hand. The coach nodded. The kid looked at me and said, "Can we be mean to him yet, or do we gotta act nice for a while?"

The coach smiled thinly. "Gerald, you know I hate nice ballplayers." He blew his two blasts on his whistle and said, "Let's go. Harold and Philippe choose teams, go shirts and skins, Philippe's go skins and take the ball first."

Well, Philippe, no doubt out of curiosity, chose me first. It's horrible to be chosen first, especially when the other team then gets to use its first pick to get Marshall. I should have been grateful I was getting my chance, but the pressure was starting to feel a little weird.

Right before we started our team circled together and Philippe said, "Start off man, go press if we get up, off guard doubles Marshall down, and on O work it weak side quick for a baseline." Then he looked at me. "I got one question."

I swallowed hard, and managed to invite it with a nod. All of them were watching me intently.

"The question is this: Do the brothers really play that hockey mess in Canada instead of hoops?"

I smiled. "Too right," I said. "Up there, it's the *game*."

"And *chicks* like you if you good? At *hockey*?"

"*Only* if you're good at hockey."

They all shook their heads in disbelief. A buzzer honked, and we jogged to our positions. I took the ball, bounced it in to Philippe, he bounced it back to me and took off upcourt, and I was underway, walking the dribble, all eyes on me.

In front of me the whole way, waving his arms aggressively, scuttling back and forth as I angled to this side or that, watching my waist with fierce concentration, was the muscular guard who had singled me out. He was all business. He flicked a hand at the ball now and then just to keep my dribble honest, but otherwise he just held perfect position. I looked dramatically at Philippe cutting along the baseline, picked up my dribble, raised the ball to my chest in both hands, and faked the pass. The high-strung guard jumped to cut off the passing lane, opening the path to my center, who was cutting by Marshall. I bounced him a simple pass and he hit a short hook.

There was some applause from the stands. My teammates slapped me and I ignored them as was the way.

At the other end Muscle-guard worked it in to Marshall and Marshall hit a ten-foot turnaround and I brought the ball up again. Their coverage got messed up and too many men were on the left side of the floor, so I decided to push it up the right and see if anything developed in our end.

It felt good to dribble and run fast. It actually felt good. I was just thinking that this might be *fun*, and was looking ahead to see my tallest forward slip behind his man and sneak to the hoop where an alley-oop would give him a slam, and I just waited for the ball to come back to my hand from the last dribble before I would whip it straight from my hip, when I realized the ball had been on the way down in that dribble for a long time now and didn't seem to be coming back. I looked down. It was gone. I turned, just in time to see Muscles leave the floor, rise about four feet, and throw down a very impressive jam for a small guy.

There were some jeers and boos from the stands. Half my teammates said things like "No sweat," and half avoided me.

From that point on, it just got worse. I shocked them all.

Oh, I made *some* plays. Once I stole a pass one of my teammates had deflected right into my face, and once I actually curled a pass behind my back because my man was overplaying me in one direction; Philippe, so startled to find the ball arriving in his gut, fumbled it away, but everyone recognized it for a good play. I hit one foul shot, and one layup. Otherwise, every single time I touched the ball, somebody suckered me into coughing it up, or I dribbled myself into a trap and had to make a terrible desperate pass that was picked off, or I simply mishandled the ball and stubbed it off my foot or shin or knee. The other team discovered pretty soon that I couldn't shoot even an eight-foot jumper, so the defenders let me penetrate and shoot, instead of dropping off their men to challenge me, thus opening up the pass I *really* had wanted to make. Three times I shot air balls from within twelve feet. Marshall blocked one of my layups with his *elbow*. My final stats: three points on 1-for-13 shooting, 1–2 from the line; three assists; an astonishing 21 turnovers, which would easily have earned me a brass piece on Coach Kantuu's plaque if this had been a real game: one steal; four fouls, though Coach Kantuu could have called twice that many if he hadn't wanted to keep me in the game, incredulously waiting for me suddenly to show up and take over.

I was easily the worst player out there. Those guys were very impressive, and they made me think much more highly of the game of hoops than I had. They worked hard, played smart, used a lot of creativity, took cool chances when they could. Before long I was more of a fan than a player.

When it became clear that I was not the player people had expected, the first reaction from the players and the fans was angry and mocking. But if you suck you have to take it, and I did. After a while, though, the players started to feel sorry for me and made efforts to cover for me, or gave me discreet tips when I did something stupid, or complimented me far too enthusiastically if I managed to complete a routine play without losing the ball. The fans turned nice, too; some of them jeered to the end, but most settled back when they realized I was not going to dazzle them, and seemed to make a special effort to withhold their scorn. Muscles, when he realized he was in no danger of losing a single minute of playing time to me, declined to become charitable, and continued to taunt me and steal me blind, but, as I said, you just have to take it if you can't cut it in the game. But at the end of the scrimmage, even Muscles showed a small glimmer of sympathy: He let me in front of him at the drinking fountain, though to mask the niceness he had to say, "Suck it up, chump, you need it worse than I do."

The only person who completely failed to see the facts was Coach Kantuu, and I am sorry to say it was ugly. He was the referee for the scrimmage, but he spent most of his time running at my elbow, cussing in disbelief when I chose to make a certain pass, yelling at me to watch out for the player about to steal the ball from me, demanding in shrill incredulity why I had not seen the open man cutting through the lane and had instead lobbed a useless pass the other way, until finally he gave up advising me and just ran alongside to give me an increasingly nasty, hissy, series of bitter put-downs. At first I tried to remind him that I had tried to keep him from expecting too much, but it was useless and I just shut up. It was clear that he took my failure very personally, as a betrayal, a mockery, a gesture of contempt.

"You dribble like a bleeping third grade girl!" he said. "What the bleep have you been *doing* all these years?"

"Playing hockey," I said, looking him in the eye (as an alert guard snatched the ball and took off).

"You haven't practiced a *thing!* You haven't worked on a single skill! You thought it would all just *be* here, didn't you?"

"Not at all," I said. "I had a very good idea it wouldn't. I just didn't care."

He almost exploded.

"As for work," I said, "I've done plenty. I've just done it on ice skates. And I can show you some pretty good skills, anytime you want to check me out in the game of *my* choice."

But talking to him wasn't worth it. Some private dream of his that had nothing to with me was getting trashed and he couldn't stop his tailspin. Finally, after I missed one open guy coming off a pick and passed instead to a forward who was double-teamed, he pulled on my shoulder until I faced him.

"Nobody makes a fool out of me," he said menacingly.

It got very quiet. He glared at me, whistled for

the ball, and restarted the scrimmage. I waited a second and kept playing. In a few minutes Coach Kantuu declared the scrimmage over.

Not quite knowing what to do, players gathered around the midcourt circle, where he was once more messing with a clipboard. Without looking up at anyone, he said, "I was under a mistaken impression earlier—in fact there *will* be cuts. See you tomorrow unless you hear different." Then he left.

The guys were really nice to me, though they were a little awkward too. I didn't hang around collecting sympathy or whining. I said, "Awesome game, Marsh," and he said, "Thanks," and then I left as if everything was normal.

Later that night, while I was waiting for my ride to the music club, Marshall called me.

"Hello," he said, as if testing the phone. He cleared his throat. "Hello."

"Don't even think about apologizing," I said. "It had nothing to do with you."

There was a brief pause. "Right," he said, and hung up.

half hour before my ride was scheduled to pick me up I knocked on the door of my grandfather's study. For a minute, he kept playing some soft, middle-register, mid-tempo chords, sounding like a lost manuscript Billy Strayhorn had written during that beautiful period right before he died. Then my grandfather's music stopped and he said, "Yes?" in the way Canadians do. Americans always say "Come in!" but to a Canadian that seems a little rude, too much like giving an order.

I opened the door and stepped in. He smiled gently up at me. "I hear you playing beautiful things all the time, Grandfather," I said, "but I never hear you singing."

"Ah," he said, and turned back to the piano. "I do most of my singing inside these days."

"But your voice is still strong and beautiful."

"Oh, my voice is fine," he said, smiling at the

keys as if in a private joke. Then, with little attitude in his eyes, he looked back up. "The voice is good. But the audience—!" He leaned his head back and laughed. It's a challenging laugh, and a visually striking one: He has never had a cavity or a filling, so all you see is white.

It took me a second to get the joke. I dropped into a low leather chair with an ottoman that he got from Lester Young's house, trading him a new pair of extremely soft shoes my grandfather had brought back from San Francisco, made of kangaroo skin.

"I guess once you've knocked 'em dead in the Rainbow Room for a few years, wearing a two-thousand-dollar tuxedo and scatting harmonies off Johnny Hodges solos, it does seem like a letdown to croon alone in Severna Park, Maryland."

"One did not scat off Mr. Hodges. He would stop playing, waiting for you to trickle to a stop, and then say 'Are you finished? May I go on with my solo?'"

I laughed, perhaps a little too hard. He smiled. "I have heard that you made an attempt to join the school basketball team today," he said.

I was taken so completely by surprise that I simply nodded.

He frowned slightly and then put his chin lightly in one hand. "And did you display the remarkable passing skills that drew so much praise during that game at Georgetown? If so, are you now to be a star on the basketball team?"

I looked at him as he calmly watched me, eyebrows slightly raised.

"I played very poorly," I said.

He nodded once, chin still in hand.

I felt the need to keep talking. "That game—that camp, the whole Georgetown thing—it was a fluke. Just a fluke."

"'A fluke,'" he said thoughtfully. "Did you know that a fluke is a fish, a flatfish not unlike the flounder? It is also a nasty parasite that grows in the livers of sheep." He made a face. Then he asked: "And basketball itself? Is that too a fluke? Or is it an interest? Or did your attempt at playing for the basketball team come about because of threats that your ice skates would be destroyed if you did not?"

Having already been surprised, I was a little more prepared for this. "Not at all," I said. "In fact, the skates were returned *before* I decided to do the basketball tryout. But how—"

"A telephone call from a very stupid young man." He shook his head.

"What did he say?"

My grandfather, like many singers, is a superb mimic. "It went something like this." He licked his lips. " 'Yo! Gimme Hokey on the horn just about now!' I informed him that you were unavailable. He continued, 'Ha! Dude be out highin'-and-lowin' for them sorry blades he missing.' I asked if he referred to my grandson's ice skates. 'You the old singin' dude? I hear you bad. Do me some tune, Pops.' I declined, and asked if he had taken your skates, and why. I also told him it would be best if he brought them back immediately. There was an explosion resembling laughter. 'He gon be have to play his next game in sneaks, like a good colored boy. You hear? That be a trip—these crackers whizzing and my homeboy out slidin' and stuff in his Rodmans. Anyway, listen up. You tell Hokey it time he did right by himself. You tell him he can't go no more thinkin' he better than everybody. Tell him he wants to play on his ice, first he got to come tomorrow and give it to us on the hardwood, baby. You got that?' I told him that in fact I did not have it at all. 'No matter. He know.' Then he hung up the telephone." My grandfather studied me as I laughed. "Tell me—did you know you would play very poorly?"

I looked at him. I shrugged. Then I nodded. "I was pretty sure. It didn't matter, though. I went and made the effort for *my* reason, and it had nothing to do with threats. I wanted to put a stop to people telling me how I was supposed to be, if I were to be myself."

My grandfather nods. "And the skates? You retrieved them with whose help?"

This was the hard part. "A guy who called me. Kind of half a composer, half a promoter."

He regarded me unblinking. "And this versatile person wanted you to do what? Make a recording? Give voice lessons to one of his protégés? Perform?"

"He wanted me to—well, to perform, but as part of an experiment in developing a new kind of music. Kind of an improvisatory kind."

"Improvisation is hardly a new kind of music,"

my grandfather said, too patiently. "Monks were doing it two thousand years ago. Is there by any chance an electronic complement to this musical adventure?"

"Yes. And please pay me the respect of not becoming sarcastic."

"Electronics. Voice. Where does one hear such music? Not by any chance in clubs known, for lack of a better word, for their programs of abhorrently loud 'pop' music, often divided into indelibly marked beats for the purpose of 'dancing'?"

"Look, Grandfather, it sounded interesting. And the guy seems smart. And I'm going to try it for half an hour tonight, so you might as well save your ultra-European, multi-syllable mockery."

"Fair enough." He nodded, and moved over to his desk. As he pulled open a couple of drawers he said, "Would you mind explaining to me how it is different to give in to the threats of a thief who is coercing you to sing, than it is to give in to those of a hooligan trying to get you to play basketball?"

I hear a car coming down the street. I knew I didn't have time for the nuances, and I doubted he'd believe me anyway right now. So as I got out of the chair I just said, "I'm surprised at you, Grandfather. When is the singing of a song not superior to the bouncing of a ball?"

"When the song is not 'sung'," he said drily, "but rather is 'bounced' as rudely as the ball. Here." He handed me a small plastic box. As the car pulled up I opened the box and found two cylindrical plugs inside.

"They are silicon," my grandfather said, pushing me toward the door. "If the drum machine and the sample loops are too loud you can roll them into balls and put them in your outer ear and still hear *plenty* well."

"Thanks," I said. By this time I was at the front door. I turned and saw him standing just outside his study. "You know, I would love to have you come, if you like."

He shook his head. "Thank you. But I'll trust you to judge your own 'experiment' first. If you find you like it—if you find you are making music— then, yes, I will be honored to come to another performance. Good night."

"Good night." He closed his door. I opened mine.

Who's got some tape?" says Barry, holding a shin guard.

"Ernie," says Dooby, taping on a shin guard of his own.

Everyone laughs. Ernie, beginning with our first practice, has carefully removed every piece of tape he used and wrapped the strips into a pure-tape sphere, solid all the way through, with a circumference that just keeps growing. We have a pool—two dollars apiece in the kitty—that will be won by the person whose guess before the first game is closest to the weight of the ball after the final game. Cody thinks the winner should get the ball, too, as does Ernie's mother. But Ernie swears he will keep the ball going for as long as he plays hockey. It is about nine inches in diameter already. He carries it in his bag, but it takes up so much room he says he's going to start bringing it in his little brother's wagon.

Dooby finishes his first shin guard and silently tosses Barry his tape. Barry silently uses it for both of his shins, and tosses it back. Dooby then tapes on his own second shin guard, all without a word.

Cody says, "It's time to play The Impossible Itch."

"Yeah," I say. "We've missed a few games."

"Oh, please, you guys—" Zip says, looking up quickly from where he kneels to fasten his second leg pad.

Cody, rubbing his chin and looking up at the clock on the wall, says, "Hmmm. Yes. Yes sir, I believe today is just one of those special days—"

"Cody, I'll really kill you," says Zip, getting nervous.

Cody looks over at me and raises three fingers, lifting his eyebrows as a question. I frown and look as if I am thinking hard, then shake my head and hold up two.

"The second period," Cody announces. "The Impossible Itch will strike in the second period of tonight's tightly fought contest, at exactly—exactly—" He closes his eyes and drops his forehead into his hand for a few seconds, then pops up with his face aglow. "At exactly 5:05! The signs have spoken! At 5:05 of the second period, way down there beneath pad and tape and pad and tape and pad and cup, out of nowhere, bursting across the skin like the bite of a thousand sand flies—"

"*Stop it!*" says Zip, grabbing one of Woodsie's skates and sawing at his pants.

"No good scratching *now*," says Woodsie, grabbing his skate back. "It won't be for a while yet . . ."

"What was the score last time we played these jerks?" asks Barry.

"One hundred to zero,"says Dooby.

"One hundred to *three*," the Boot corrects in a flat voice. "The Boot had the hat trick, though the rest of you were useless."

Barry nods. "They beat us pretty good." He leans over to pull a stocking over his right foot. "Maybe it will be a little different this time."

"Yeah," says Dooby. "Maybe the Boot will only get a pair."

"The Boot does not regress," says the Boot.

Cody looks thoughtful. "We could *win*," he says. Then: "Or, we could *lose*."

"Genius!"

"Leadership!"

"The willingness to take a stand!"

"It's that firm, decisive spirit one admires so much in a captain," says Woodsie.

"Well, he *did* decide we couldn't *tie*," Dooby points out. "Next, you'll expect him to predict a score or something."

"Seven to three," says Cody. "Def."

"I think Cody's right," says Ernie. "That will be the final score. And I can see how it happens." He leans forward and drops his voice. "It's three–three, anybody's game, next goal wins; even though it's only the second period, we all *feel* it, the game is on the line right now. Then, a seemingly harmless pass skips over one of our sticks and winds up on the blade of their fourth-line center, that kid with one eye that always looks sideways, remember?, and he can barely skate and doesn't even want to, but he kind of lumbers in on Zip, real clumsy, and Zip's looking sharp, and we're all thinking 'No prob, when's the next line change?' when—yes!—somebody looks up at the clock, and it's ticking as the center stumbles closer, 5:08, 5:07, the kid pulls back his stick and starts a klutzy swing, Zip is set but something's wrong, 5:06 . . ."

"*Yaaaaaaah!*" screams Zip, and runs into the bathroom.

Ah, it is great to be back with a hockey team.

Yesterday's basketball fiasco seems like part of a different life. For a better reason, so does last night's "musical experiment." It turned out that the promoter I spoke to is a young lawyer from Annapolis, named Melton. His hobby is collecting and rebuilding old Casio keyboards and Roland machines and even a couple of theremins, all of which he hooks up to a computer and feeds from a breathtaking record collection that lets him put his finger on any sound imaginable to accompany a singer's improvised lyrics. I was nervous at the idea of making up stuff, but Melton explained that it wasn't like hip-hop, with strict rhymes and rhythms. Melton worked beats into his music by repeating little note patterns, not by clanging a drum machine.

"Tell some stories," he said. "Sing some non-sense." I started just half talking, half singing about

Canada, and Melton backed me with wild windy sounds and watery runs; then I got onto my grandfather for a while, and he put together this layered, sequenced medley of swing tunes, some of them actually using my grandfather's records; and then, without really knowing how it happened, I found myself really going on the subject of ice hockey— the speed, the ice, the sound of the blades, the feel of getting whacked hard and knowing it can't reach you through your pads, the flow of five guys wheeling at once, and glory of glories—the pass. Melton, whipping through discs and tapes and keyboards, made a soundtrack to the whole thing, and by the time it was over all these very cool people were listening, some dancing a little but listening too. Then they clapped. I turned and clapped for Melton but he was too lost in wires and records to acknowledge it, so I stood up off my stool and bowed.

My grandfather was waiting up for me. I told him it went well. He was cranky. I told him I was planning on getting into it deeper, but that he could always verify the safety of the clubs and all that. "What about the safety of music?" he snorted, and I decided not to ruin a good night by arguing, so I went to bed and left him muttering downstairs.

Coach Cooper comes in and says, "Frenchy! Prince! Favor us with a tune, if you please!"

I stand on a bench and sing "Things Ain't What They Used to Be." When I finish it is quiet, until Cody says, "Let us pray . . ."

Barry stands up and says, "Tie your skates, girls. Let's get out there and see if these yuppies have shrunk any since the last time we played them."

Ten minutes later, lined up across from a center eight inches taller than I am and probably forty pounds heavier, I regret to conclude that they haven't shrunk at all. If anything, I think to myself as I check out this monster, they've gotten—

"Hey!" I say to the kid. "Were you in the game last time?"

He grins behind his cage, showing an electric green tooth guard, and shakes his head.

"We like to hold back a few surprises for the second time around," their right winger says. He leans closer and speaks behind his glove. "And don't look now or anything, but we brought two fresh defensemen who are almost the same size." He winks. "In the spirit of good clean fun for us all."

A minute later, when the ref drops the puck, I dart right past it and pop smack into the big guy. His head is down as he fishes at the puck, and he goes right over onto his back pretty hard before he knows what's going on. It's an illegal check but I get away with it because I'm small. Meanwhile, behind the ref's back, Cody chops the chatty right winger's stick to the ice and gives it a little slide backwards to the boards.

I just keep skating straight between their defensemen and look down just before I cross the blue line and the puck appears, passing *between my skates* no less, at the perfect pace, leading me just onside full speed at their goalie. I fake a forehand and he bites, then I swerve the other way and lift in a soft backhander—and we have picked up where we left off. I hear some cheers. A couple of Wings rub my helmet.

"Nice look, Woodsie," I holler.

"Who says it was me?" he says, acting all innocent.

"Had your name written all over that pass. Between my *skates.*"

"You liked that?" he says. "I thought you'd see it better in front of you that way."

"Show-off."

After the second face-off the big center throws *me* down, but Cody whizzes through and picks up the puck and Boot scoots in to trail. I pull myself up by holding the big guy's stick shaft and he says, "Hey, asswipe—" and I skate after them. As Cody crosses the blue line one of their fresh big defensemen throws his body into a huge disguised check that knocks Cody completely off his skates but also leaves the defenseman out of the play, because at the last second Cody drops a pass Boot picks up perfectly, and Woodsie jumps up into the play and we have a two-on-one. Boot fakes the pass and shoots (of course) and the goalie makes an awkward save that leaves the puck spinning just out of his reach in the low slot. I just manage to get there ahead of three of their players, and chip it over the goalie, and we are *up*. I have never scored two on one shift before, so I give a few pumps with the right arm and skate one-footed through the corner and back up ice. Woodsie and Barry mug me. And this time I hear some *heavy* cheering, from the stands, with a few whoops thrown in.

"Change," hollers Coach Coop. As Dooby skates past me onto the ice he says, "What did you do, win the spelling bee at school or something?"

"What do you mean?"

He tilts his head toward the stands on the far side of the ice. "Check it out. And we had *so* hoped to keep it from you that you were from a different ethnic group than the rest of us."

I climb onto the bench and sit between Cody and Boot and look up at the stands. The two of them are already looking there.

"Wow," says Cody, delicately. "New crowd."

"Diversity at last," says Boot.

Up high in the seats, in a rough block about even with the red line, there must be twenty black kids, some of them still clapping. This is a night game, so there are more of the usual parents than is common, but even so there aren't more than twenty-five of them altogether, scattered around. A few are looking discreetly up at the mass of 'new crowd' and no doubt wondering, as am I, what is going on.

"This is it, guys," I say. "Power to the *People*. We're taking over."

On the ice one of their big wingers barrels past the bench, carrying the puck along the boards. Dooby, backskating, suddenly cuts a hip into him perfectly, pinning him while Barry calmly collects the puck as it trickles ahead into the corner. Cody and I holler *"Good hit"* at Doobs, but we are almost drowned out by the cheering from the black kids.

"No doubt you explained offside and icing to them," says Cody. "Their grasp of the subtleties, and all that."

"It doesn't take much to like a hit like that," I say. "But seriously—I kind of know some of those kids, but I don't have any idea . . ."

"Marshall might have brought them," says Cody.

"But Marshall is just walking in now," says Boot, pointing.

Indeed, there is my skinny friend hulking as he enters the building through a glass door under the stands. He slinks toward the stairs that lead to the stands, hands in pockets, deep hood pulled all the way forward.

"*He's* having fun, at least," says Cody. The black group sees Marshall and hollers and waves him up. To my surprise, he begins the climb to join them.

"Change," Coach Cooper says.

"Us," says Cody, hustling over the boards.

"See if you can get three this shift, Prince," says the coach.

"Certainly," I say. "The Prince would hate to regress."

Their coach has made a change, however, and now I find myself facing a center I remember from the last game. He is smaller than the monster from the first shift, but, as I recall, he is a much better skater, passer, and defender. Plus, he isn't all *that* much smaller. He wins the face-off and gives me a good bump as he skates past and beats me into the zone. The defenseman who got the puck has whipped it wide to the left wing who crosses a step ahead of the center. Woodsie forces the winger way wide but he manages to sling a blind, lucky centering pass through Woodsie's skates. I am behind the center as he takes it and I get my stick under his but my leverage isn't good enough to lift it. Ernie, facing the center, thinks for a moment too long and ends up standing still as the guy cuts by him and jams the puck through Zip's pads.

"Gee," says Zip to the guy. "You're *strong*." Then he looks at Woodsie, who is scooping the shameful puck out of the net. "And *you're* unlucky," he says. "So please get off my ice now."

"Sorry, Zip," says Woodsie.

"My fault," says Ernie.

"I should have caught him," I say.

"Well, boo-bleeping-hoo," says Zip. "We're all just so sad." He whacks me in the shinguards with his stick. "Go get another goal, you moron. You guys can cry later."

"Right."

I hear some noise from the stands as I skate to center, and look over. About six of the kids are standing up and looking hard at Zip. "No," I say, involuntarily, "it's okay, see—"

"Glad you liked it, buttface," says a voice, and I look back down and find the center grinning. "If you liked that one, I'll do it again."

I win the face-off and get by him, but Ernie loses the puck in his skates and their right winger, who this time has thrown *Cody* down behind the ref's back, tips it free and breaks in on Zip. Woodsie, coming from the other side, dives headlong at the last possible second with his stick stretched full out and *just* tips the puck away enough to mess up the guy's control, and he fans on the shot.

What a play. As he lands on his stomach and slides, Woodsie lets his stick slip out of his grasp. The ref blows his whistle.

Incredibly, he calls "throwing the stick," and points to the middle, for a penalty shot.

We are all screaming at him and following him as he picks up the puck and skates to place it on the center of the red line. Coach Cooper is hollering from the bench, *"Sir, please, sir, a word"* with loud politeness, which is what he does when he is really, really angry. Woodsie stands in the corner, unable to believe it, until the ref whistles at him and waves him out to get behind the red line.

"Great play, Woodsie," hollers the coach. *"You got the puck clean."*

"That's enough," says the ref, pointing at Coach Coop. Then he turns to the winger, who is waiting to start. He nods. "Go," he says. "One shot."

We all have to stand behind the play and watch.

Zip says he'd rather face one player he can concentrate on, no matter how good his moves are, than a screened shot from the point that hits a hip and two skates before it gets to him. But he's probably changed his mind at least this once, because the winger gets him to drop to his knees and fires it in off the top of Zip's right shoulder, and we are tied.

My big shift is history—it's a brand new hockey game.

But maybe not really, because as we skate by to tap Zip I can see that he's losing it a little. He's screaming stupid mad stuff behind his mask and whacking both goalposts with his stick behind his back. I start to skate up to him but Cody whizzes by me, stops in a spray that covers Zip from chin to skates, and grabs his jersey.

"Shut up," Cody says. "Shut up now and concentrate. You hear me?"

"Kiss my—"

"Shut up now and concentrate, or I'll make your nads itch," Cody says.

Zip suddenly moans. "No, Cody, jeez—"

Cody lets go of the jersey and skates away. "He's okay," he says as he passes me.

We play the rest of the period tied.

During the break, while Coach gives us a quick lecture on the futility of trying to check bigger guys high, and the goalies skate slowly to switch ends, I get more time to look up into the stands. I don't believe what I see: by now there must be forty black kids up there together, the ones on the edges of the group chatting away with nearby team parents, the ones at the top sitting motionless on the poles that are there, peering from the shadows beneath their caps with their sweatshirt hoods up, their hands in the pockets of their White Sox and Jaguar and Raider jackets.

"Some of those are *high* school guys," Dooby says quietly beside me.

I nod. I look at individuals, one by one, and before we take the ice again I have spotted seven members of the basketball team, and, in the middle of them, Coach Kantuu. Other kids I recognize; not many are what I would call my better friends.

Zip apparently spotted the group as he skated to the other cage, and as we circle past him now to tap his pads he holds both fists in the air.

"The Revolution has come!" he barks. "The

Revolution!" He points his stick at the Reston bench. "The saggy old tired imperialist culture that spawned you inbred yuppie idiots is *over, do you hear me? Over! The new era of rough-ass harmony, hip-hop and hockey together as one, it's here, you Volvo-850-driving pigs!*"

"Excuse me, goalie," the ref calls from center. "Are you ready?"

"Sure," says Zip, whacking the poles behind him. "I've been ready for years. I have guns under my bed, I have a Classics Illustrated of *The Autobiography of Malcolm X*, I eat Thai food, I did not allow my parents to take imperialistic snapshots of my Native American brothers who were posing everywhere in their unjust degradation when we visited Santa Fe last year. . . ."

The puck drops. I hook it back to Woodsie, slip by their center, swing wide, cross the blue line as Woodsie carries it in along the far boards, then curl back between the defensemen who are watching him, and the next thing you know, here's the puck arriving with some zip and I'm still untouched between the two hulks. I time a tight spin so that as the puck passes I swat it along its same path with a blind backhand, and it hits the inside of the far post and angles nicely in.

"Here we bleeping go again," says one defenseman, giving me a half-hearted cross check. I lift my arms, Ernie jumps me from behind and Cody grabs me from in front and Woodsie rubs my helmet, and I hear Zip screaming *"See? It's over!"* but he is drowned out by a huge whooping and clapping and stomping from the new crowd in the stands. I look up and see Dooby's mom explaining something to a kid, and he turns around and hollers to the group, and the next thing you know everybody wearing a hat or cap, even the badass gangstahs on the back rail, has run down to the glass and thrown the piece of headwear over onto the ice. It is the first time I have seen a hat trick celebrated correctly since Mites.

"Change!" hollers the coach and I barely hear him, and head for the bench. I am watching the crowd. Coach Kantuu is actually standing and shaking a fist.

"Now, don't cry, sweetheart," says Dooby as he skates by.

"Pretty shot, Princer," says Coach Cooper, tapping my helmet.

"*Greedy* shot," says Woodsie, climbing behind me. "It was going in anyway."

"You wish. But it *was* a fabulous pass."

"Well, keep your eyes open," he says.

"Yeah," Cody whines, "but, like, what about the special telepathic blind-passing bond between Prince—the passer, the great *playmaker*, remember?—and *me*—the swift and deceptive pure goal scorer? I mean, am I ever going to see the puck again?"

"And who might you be?" Woodsie asks.

On the ice, Shark, anchored unsteadily in the high slot, swings at a passing puck and redirects it in between the goalie's skates. Another eruption. Several players on the bench whack their sticks against the boards and chant "*Spaz! Spaz! Spaz!*" On the ice Shark tries to whirl his arm into the pump, loses his balance, and falls down.

"*Spaz! Spaz! Spaz!*"

"They're toast," says Cody calmly, watching the Reston players change lines.

"Yup."

But maybe not quite. We score another—by Barry, who was just trying to fire the puck back into the slot from the point, but it hit a skate and went in, profoundly embarrassing him in his defensive purity—and then another—Cody, unassisted, off a poke check while he was backchecking for Ernie, who had fallen down—but then, just before the period ends, they get one back on a tremendous high shot from the point that a forward in the slot tips so that it dives from waist level to the ice, under Zip's blocker. They go into the break with a little boost.

In our bunch-up at the bench, Coach says, "Hey—remember when we decided to clamp down and take that tie?"

"*Yes!*" we yell.

"Was that some tremendous team hockey we played in that third period, or *what*?"

"*Yes!*" we yell.

"Well?" he says. "Do we want to clamp down now, cut their hearts out by stopping every desperate thing they try, make 'em start taking penalties out of frustration, *now*, with a *three-goal lead*? Do we want to do that?"

"*No!*" we yell.

He blinks for a second. "Well, okay then," he

says. "Go ahead and beat them *worse.*"

On the fourth shift Cody scores off a no-look magic-feed from me. On the shift after that, Billy scores a beauty off a pass from Allround. The lead is five. *Now* we decide to clamp down, and they get frustrated and nasty and start taking some dumb penalties and we just pass the puck around on the power play all night, like keep-away, until with four seconds left Dooby casually slings it at the goal and it goes just under the crossbar.

We win by six. Two in a row. We collapse on Zip, who, I would bet, is foaming at the mouth inside his mask.

The stands are shaking. I look over in between handshakes in the line, and see my grandfather slapping five with a hip-hop eighth-grader in a wool stocking cap pulled down to his eyes and baggies with the waist so low they show a good foot of his boxer shorts. Marshall is standing up, clapping mildly, no expression on his face. Coach Kantuu is down at the glass, tapping. I wave and he waves, then makes a fist, then leaves. I look around. It would be too much if Muscles, the kid who whupped my tail yesterday, were here, but he's not.

I don't know half of the kids tipping me nods.

The locker room is pretty rambunctious. I am forced to sing three songs, one for each goal of my hat trick, and then I am forced to do an encore. I am slightly off-pitch at the end of the encore. Then Zip and Dooby, dressed in only their cups but with hats of long hockey stockings pulled top-end over their heads down to their mouths, stand on a bench and deliver a very clever tit-for-tat rap with Boot tapping a backbeat, and Dooby rhymes "lascivious" with "mischi(e)vious" to great applause.

Barry watches it all, cranky. Taking off a skate, he says, to no one in particular, "Well, our record still sucks."

"Maybe," I say. "We could use a few more wins, and we're gonna probably lose a bunch more too. But there's one thing we got now that we won't ever lose."

"What?" he asks grumpily.

"This team," I announce, "officially has *soul*."

Here's a sneak peek at the next book in the
Wolfbay Wings ice hockey
series by Bruce Brooks

SHARK

available from HarperCollins

am an ice hockey player. I go by the name of Shark.

Pretty easy to remember, isn't it? Pretty cool image to carry around. A twisting torpedo of writhing muscle. Keen with that alertness that makes intelligence seem slow. Roaming relentlessly, sharp-toothed, fight-ready, eager to slash at the slightest opening, with no conscience, no mercy, leaving no remains.

Shark. Kind of says a lot about a guy, especially when that name is chosen for him, by a bunch of tough, gritty, hardass ice hockey players who don't hand out favors to anybody.

Shark. It's a name I earned for one reason, then lost, then earned again for another. That's hard. That's work.

How did I earn it first, this name of speed and death and grace? It was easy. I earned it by being the fattest, slowest, most confused hockey player on my team, the Wolfbay Wings Squirt A's. When I tried to stickhandle, I often lost the puck and my stick as well. At least twice a game I would get spun around and my "ice sense" would tell me my team was supposed to head in the direction that was actually reserved for our opponents. I once shot on my own goalie (missed the net, but I worried him for a minute). My idea of defense was managing to drag an opponent to the ice with me as I frequently fell; my idea of playing team offense was managing to skate at least three strides (without the puck, of course) in the right direction, without going offside. I was awesome.

So the nickname was a kind of joke, as was the general name for the four or five of us who had been recruited to fill empty roster spots, and had no business on skates holding hard sticks with which we very well might injure ourselves: we were the Spazzes, or sometimes, the Spaz Line. Yes, it was a joke, but let me tell you, it was also a badge of honor. Because when I took the ice—and all of us Spazzes skated regular shifts, same as the stars—I took it without apology, without resignation, without shame. I took the ice—even in full wobble—

with pride, buddy. I was a Wolfbay Wing. I wore the blue and black and white; I was one of the first three on the ice at every practice and one of the last three to leave; I worked my fins off, and if the results didn't show much at first, who cared? I was playing hockey. And one day—who could say?— one day maybe I was going to eat me some people.

But as I said, before then I had my much-treasured name cruelly taken from me by the same teammates who gave it the first time. Did that *hurt*? Oh, it hurt all right. But I had to remember the vital fact about sharks: They never stop moving, never, always swimming every second, from birth to death.

Here's the story of all this tough swimmin', and how close one fat fish came to bringing it all to a very bad end and—who knows?—suffering through *next* year being called something like "Bait."

two

Because I play on a sports team now, I get to spend a lot of time with kids who, you know, just *play sports*— grew up playing sports, watched big brothers and sisters play sports, lived in houses full of sports trophies with the arms broken off, wore hand-me-down sports jerseys as plain shirts, could reach down in the middle of any floor and come up with a piece of sports equipment that they would know how to hold and handle without thinking— kids who got driven to practices and games all the time, driving that takes up twelve to twenty hours a week, by parents who just expected to do it, who shrugged and started the van and didn't imagine any other way to live—hey, the kids do *sports*, okay?

And once you notice sports, you start seeing sports *everywhere*. Open a magazine and there are pictures of ragamuffin kids in Bangladesh or Liverpool or a slum of Brisbane carrying on a soccer game with a misshapen ball made of waste from the local emergency starvation clinic, kids intent and competitive and smiling and—*goal!* Turn on your television and get sold some $200 sneakers; fold back a long, dignified page of *The Wall Street Journal* and get sold a seat at an international marketing conference with a star athlete as the keynote speaker.

It's hard for my teammates to believe what I am about to reveal, but it is the plain truth/incredible as it sounds: It is possible for a kid—even a *boy*—to get to the age of ten in this country without ever having hit a baseball with a bat or a tennis ball with a racket, caught a spiraling football or a bouncing basketball, kicked a soccer ball—and you can even grow up without even *wanting* to do these things.

It doesn't happen because the kid is a scaredy nerd, a sissy, an uncoordinated doofus who can barely walk up a flight of stairs, a computer geek, or a wuss without a clue about what really matters in life. I mean there are plenty of scaredy cats and doofuses and sissies around, and they live the way they have to live, sports or no sports. But sometimes a kid who, given the chance, might really *like* sports just doesn't get a peek at that world.

In my case, as for most other sports-free kids, it was a matter of what my parents knew about and cared about. My father is a Methodist minister, a good man who reads a lot of Bible, a book in which there is very little written about soccer. My mother used to be a minor opera singer; there are very few operas about basketball. My mom developed a program for training church choirs at a very successful summer camp held just for that purpose every year. During their downtime, the kids at her camp do other things besides play catch. I'm not there to play Ping-Pong, anyway, I'm working my tail off on "staff," washing dishes or assembling risers or photocopying sheet music or fitting seventy seven music stands into a single Mitsubishi van. I'm not chillin' in front of the tube in the dorm watching the O's do something called "three-hit" the Toronto Blue Jays . . .

I was riding in a car once with a kid whose dad, with great focus and precision, was explaining to him—at about age seven—the difference between a curveball and a slider. How the ball was held for each, how the pitcher moved his hand, wrist, elbow, shoulder, how the pitch looked coming to the plate, how it cut into the air and made its last-second deviation from the expected path. . . . It took about half an hour and the kid listened intently and asked very specific questions. The father answered carefully. It seemed pretty serious for both of them.

Well, I'm certain neither of my parents could tell me the difference between a curveball and a slider. I'd be surprised if they could tell me the difference between a baseball and a softball, even if I spotted them the color of the stitches. I can imagine them thinking, "Heavens, is *every* toss and catch and step and swing measured and analyzed like that?" And upon learning the answer was "Oh, absolutely!" they would just think, "But—*why?*"

If you like your life, you're about as lucky as you can get. So you don't need to go further and worry about what *kind* of life you're enjoying, and what kind you are *not*. You can't really figure it out anyway; the lines that mark this life from that aren't so clear. If I were a little less alert, I could be excused for being *shocked* at how many families out there don't know a perfect fifth held three measures with vibrato from a diminished fifth faded over three measures without vibrato. It just depends on who you get for parents.

My mother made sure I had the chance to listen to a lot of music as a kid, and I really took to it for reasons I actually do not remember anymore. Somehow I decided at an alarmingly early age that I wanted to play the oboe. So the oboe became my "extra thing" aside from schoolwork (I go to a church school) and church activities and friendships. I took oboe lessons, played recitals, went to music camps, entered music competitions, traveled with an orchestra, went through six different teachers, got to beat the absolute living crud, oboe to oboe, out of a snakehearted rival who had been mean and cocky to me for three years—listen, I had a ball. I just never *threw* one.

Then one spring I applied to a very prestigious summer study program. The application process involved three recitals, one of them in front of a world-famous conductor named Daniel Barenboim, which I aced, and two interviews.

As the date for acceptances neared, my parents grew nervous. Then my mother received a very unusual phone call. The director of the program happened to be in town seeing to some business about grants, and he wondered if she could spare him half an hour in his hotel's coffee shop. Astonished, she agreed to go.

The headmaster, she later reported, was very gracious, and bought her a pot of tea, after inquiring if she preferred herbal; he also offered her a pastry, which she declined. Then he had a nice, long, frank talk with her about me. Basically, he explained that my musicianship and what he called my "general character" made me a "very fine" candidate for the program. But, he regretted to say, the decision of the admissions committee had been to defer acceptance for a year, possibly two.

Why? asked my mom, completely perplexed.

Because, the headmaster explained, no doubt very delicately, he and the head of the winds faculty really thought I would benefit from a life in which I did something besides play the skinny horn and go to church.

My mother says she then knew two things at once: first, that I would never be a particularly special musician, because these people want *those* kids to give up everything *but* their instrument; and, second, she knew the director was right about my life, and that she and my dad would have no idea what to do about it.

I won't go through all of the comical attempts my parents made in a spirit of total willingness and beneficence to allow me to choose some new activity that would broaden my experience of the well-rounded oboist's life. You'll get an idea of how far they were prepared to go when I tell you that my father, the Methodist minister whose idea of a hot night is an impassioned discussion of Solomon with two of his younger "radical" deacons, took me to a full-blown superstar-lineup big-wheel-truck demolition derby in an arena filled with shrieking rednecks. *And* bought me a red cap with yellow letters on it that said MY WHEELS ARE BIGGER THAN YOUR HOUSE. I never had the heart to wear it.

One day one of the mothers who drive my music-lesson carpool got messed up in her scheduling, and had to stop on the way home to pick up her younger son, who was just finishing his ice hockey practice at a nearby rink. Probably because I didn't want to spend any time alone with her daughter, a snooty violinist, I decided to dash in with the mother as she picked up her kid.

It was like seeing the ocean for the first time. Or mountains. Or your very first comic book.

I'm sure my mouth dropped open and did not shut until I was somehow guided back to the car.

I arrived home and announced to my parents that my horizons were at last about to broaden. When I told them what I wanted to do, I think my father, at least, was relieved. My mother was puzzled. But the fact that I would at least have to learn to ice-skate gave her something to be pleased about. So I had their full support. They started The Project of finding me a team right away. And, as I have already explained, I was lucky enough to end up a Wing.

Now, if only I could remember why I used to like that oboe so much. . . .

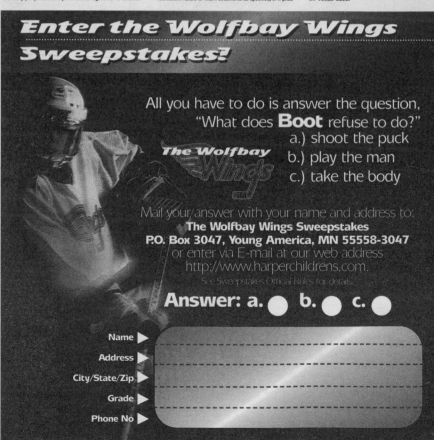